Out of the Blue

MARK BARITA

TRAFFORD

• Canada · UK · Ireland · USA •

Note for Librarians: A cataloguing record for this book is available from Library and Archives
Canada at www.collectionscanada.ca/amicus/index-e.html
ISBN 1-4120-9168-3

♻ green power

Printed in Victoria, BC, Canada. Printed on paper with minimum 30% recycled fibre.
Trafford's print shop runs on "green energy" from solar, wind and other environmentally-friendly power sources.

TRAFFORD
PUBLISHING™

Offices in Canada, USA, Ireland and UK

Book sales for North America and international:
Trafford Publishing, 6E–2333 Government St.,
Victoria, BC V8T 4P4 CANADA
phone 250 383 6864 (toll-free 1 888 232 4444)
fax 250 383 6804; email to orders@trafford.com
Book sales in Europe:
Trafford Publishing (UK) Limited, 9 Park End Street, 2nd Floor
Oxford, UK OX1 1HH UNITED KINGDOM
phone +44 (0)1865 722 113 (local rate 0845 230 9601)
facsimile +44 (0)1865 722 868; info.uk@trafford.com
Order online at:
trafford.com/06-0922

10 9 8 7 6 5 4

OUT OF THE BLUE

Chapter 1

IT WAS a warm, sunny day, in early September, and Michael was making his way through the crowded halls toward the exit door of the school. The dismissal bell had just rung and it was finally time to head home. Just as he reached for the handle to push the door open he paused, he realized he had forgotten his math book in his locker. He looked back toward his locker and then to the outside. He felt the door pull at him, beckon him to go through it and into the world outside.

He started to turn toward the door when he heard a voice in his head say, "Is your homework finished?"

He looked back at his locker, but the pull of the outside had him and dragged him away from the building and into the bright afternoon sun. His math book was still in his locker and that is where it would stay. School was over and that was all that mattered to him at this point. He knew he would have to answer to his parents about not having his homework done, but he would just make up a story like he always did.

As he made his way from the school and down the sidewalk toward his house, he was enjoying the warm afternoon sun when he thought he heard something. A strange, wind noise, a kind of a howling, but it was gone. He then sensed something, but wasn't sure what it was.

The sky was crystal clear and the sun was bright. He looked up and squinted into the glare, but saw nothing. He just shook his head and continued home. He sometimes would see things that weren't there or hear something no one else did. He figured this must just be one of those times.

Suddenly, he felt a wave of air coming toward him from his back. He wasn't sure what it was at first, and didn't know if he should turn around. The hair on his neck began to stand up and his ears were searching to find the sound again. Before he knew it, his whole body was in a shadow. He stood frozen in his steps, slowly turning to look behind him not sure what to expect.

Then, as if time and sound were standing still, he saw it. Two F-16 fighter planes came screaming over his head, only about two-hundred feet in the air. He was nearly knocked to the ground by the compression wave from the jets. The sound then caught up to them and was loud and roaring and hurt his ears and made him jump.

He watched them as they climbed into the blue, afterburners shooting fire and the sound was deafening. He was trembling and his skin was all goose bumpily from the fright he had just endured.

He looked skyward at the planes as they climbed away and screamed, "Are you trying to give me a heart attack, dad?"

While he watched them, they circled in the distance

and then came back around and over his head again, wings swaying up and down. Right then he knew his dad was back at his old tricks. Michael's dad was always messing around like this and it seemed like every time he had a chance he was buzzing their house, their mom, or him.

"I'll get you tonight!" He yelled at the planes as they flew off into the distant sky.

Michael then composed himself and continued to walk home. As he did he kept one eye on the sky, so he wouldn't be caught by surprise again.

Michael was like any other eleven year old in the early stages of the twenty-first century. He would struggle through school each day only to return home and have to try his best to complete his homework, which he always thought was too much. Michael was working his way through the very difficult middle school experience of the sixth grade. Like any other sixth grader, he was also reaching that critical time of being a pre-teen. This was not sitting well with his mother who was beginning to worry that her little boy was growing up. She wasn't really thrilled at the attitude he seemed to be getting as he got older, and how he didn't put a lot of effort into school or anything else he was doing.

Michael's life had begun on the other side of the country. He had spent most of his first eleven years growing up in the hot desert southwest. He liked it there, because he had a swimming pool he could use ten months of the year. But, there were things he also didn't like, the heat, and of course the school work. Michael believed then, as he does now, that children should get to choose whether or not they wanted to go to school.

3

He now lived with his family in a small town. This was different from what he had been used to. It was easy for him to get to school, since it was just a short walk from his home. He was happy about that, as he had come to really dislike riding on the overcrowded, uncomfortable school bus in the big city.

His family was living in the humid, wooded, East Coast near the Nations Capital, Washington, DC. The jobs were better there and he was closer to the rest of his relatives, grandparents, and aunts. At least that is what his parents had told him. He really wasn't sure why they had moved all of the way across the country. Like most other things in his life he just had to accept it.

His parents were both school teachers, which made his near failing grades that much more of an issue at dinner. His younger sister, Michelle, whom he loved to aggravate, was in the fourth grade. She was getting good grades and passing all of her tests. This seemed to add to Michael's frustrations. It seemed like no matter how hard he tried, he just couldn't do as good in school as she was doing.

Then there was his other little sister, a doll from China. Kimberly was her name and she was like a statue, a baby doll, whom he loved very much. She had straight black hair that just glowed. Her eyes were like the blackest pearls in the sea. Her smile was as wide and bright as any he had seen. She had been adopted by his family about two years ago. He wasn't sure about it at first, as he had always wanted a brother. However, looking at her now, she was everything he could ever have asked for. He wouldn't trade her for anything. She loved him very much and he loved her back.

He soon learned to enjoy his new home and his new life.

He liked to explore the forest behind his house where he could hunt for frogs. There was a small stream that flowed through it and it was full of wild life. Frogs where his passion and he would go out every day to try to catch and name them. His sister, Michelle, thought he was kind of goofy about frogs and toads but she liked to see them when he would catch them. Michael knew that Michelle couldn't catch them herself, so he liked to show off his skill to her. Kimberly just enjoyed having an older brother around who could catch the hopping frogs. He was her hero and she adored him. He just would never admit to it.

Michael also enjoyed building things, which came in handy in his new house. His mom and dad where doing some remodeling and his dad would always let Michael help out. Even though he would mess things up and get in the way, his dad still liked to have him around while he was working. His dad also liked to talk to Michael. He liked to tell him stories and show him how to do things. But most of the time Michael would just be daydreaming or doing his own thing and would not be listening.

Michael is very creative and he would always find a way to make things out of the scraps or even the tools his dad was using. This seemed to be fun until he would be making something out of his dad's tools when his dad needed one. It was always the same thing, he would get into trouble and be sent away to do something else, not knowing why.

He also had a dad who was into airplanes, being a pilot that was a given, and Michael would help him build his model airplanes.

"He has one huge model of a World War II plane! It's controlled by radios and my dad flies it." He would always brag to his friends.

"And someday it will be mine to fly…, and crash!" He would joke.

That was one reason he wasn't allowed to fly it now. Like most children his age, it was more fun to crash the plane and watch it burn, than to make a perfect landing. His dad was trying to teach him some of the flying techniques so he could someday use them. But, as usual, his mind was always on something else, and he would very rarely get it right. Once again he would be sent off to do something else.

This lack of understanding to detail and his attention span could just be blamed on him being a child. Michael claims it was a product of his childhood in the deserts of Nevada. He had been born during a full moon and on Halloween. Those were two things his mother always pointed out when he acted silly or strange. He would just tell everyone that the sun was frying his brain. Even though he knew it was not possible, there were a few times when his parents thought he might try to test that theory… on his sister.

Growing up in Las Vegas was not very exciting for him. Oh sure, he had his friends and family, but something always seemed to be missing. He was too young to gamble and the buffets just weren't his style. So he would just spend all of his free time building Lego's, swimming, and arguing with his sisters. But that was what was leaving him with the feeling of needing more, being more, and the feeling that he had something important to do in the world.

He never paid much attention to what his parents did for a living. He knew they went to work each day and would talk about school at night. His mother taught at an elementary school and his dad was at a university. That was about all he knew. This was something he would come to understand later.

Being a teen now, or close to one, had begun to change him a little, and he was starting to understand his life more. He was starting to see that his parents were sometimes right and that his sisters weren't always wrong, and that he needed to close the bathroom door when he was using it.

His sister would say he left it open because he was afraid of being alone. But that wasn't true, maybe he was just lazy. He wasn't afraid of anything!

Michael always had a feeling that there was something he was looking for, but he didn't know what it was, and it seemed to still be too far away for him to find. One day he started to have feelings he couldn't explain and then they were gone. Almost like a vision of something he had to do. He was right on the edge of this new power, this understanding of his place in the world. However, it was still just out of his reach.

As time passed he learned more about life in this new century and how different it was from what his parents had seen as children. He remembered some of the stories his dad would tell him about his childhood. Like how his dad wouldn't get a toy every time they went to the store, like he did now. He really had a problem understanding how his dad lived without a Dollar Store.

He also didn't understand how those wonderful, nice grandparents of his were so mean to his dad. This, he couldn't believe, since he loved his grandparents so much and they treated him so well.

He could remember how many gifts they would bring him when they would visit him in Nevada. He loved to go to their house and play with all his dad's old toys and trains. He liked how the house smelled, both inside and out. Grandma was always cooking something and she made the best cakes.

During his visits, she would always make him whatever he wanted for breakfast. She would serve him in front of the TV while he watched his favorite shows on Nickelodeon and Cartoon Network. Michael even once commented to his dad that he must have felt like the luckiest little kid growing up with a mother who let him eat in front of the TV.

"As if that really happened." His dad would say.

One time on a visit there, his grandpa even let him back the car out of the driveway. He thought that was really cool! He told his dad he was ready to get his license. Once again his dad would just laugh and tell him to go play.

One of the favorite things for him to do there was to chase squirrels. He was an outdoor person and loved the wildlife. He would try and sneak up on them and then watch them scamper up a tree or run through the grass. One time he actually got close enough to catch one in a net, if he had had one.

On this day, as he stood looking out the window at a rain shower, he began to understand more about his life. He always thought he must have a special gift, a type of super power. He just wasn't sure what it was or how to use it.

Looking into the rain he began to see how the world was changing. He had heard of how much his parents had struggled to get to this point in their life. He also remembered hearing something on the news each day about a place called Iraq. He would listen to his parents complain about the price of gas and food. This all seemed to be of no consequence to him until he started to think about it a little more.

"Maybe that is why I didn't get that new computer game I wanted?"

This was just one of the many questions that seemed to fill his thoughts as he gazed out of the window.

Soon, his thoughts turned back to why it was raining on a day off from school? He couldn't believe how nice the weather was all week, and now on the weekend, when he had so much to do outside, it was raining.

It was at that moment that the phone rang. His dad looked at him, he looked back at his dad. Was he supposed to answer the phone? He was closest to it, so he took the responsibility for answering it knowing full well it was probably not for him.

"Hello" he said in the disinterested voice of an eleven year old.

The voice on the other end replied, "Hi Michael, and how are you doing today?"

"Fine," was about all he could get out. Michael did not like to talk on the phone.

"What is your dad doing?"

"I don't know."

His dad, sitting on the couch watching a football game, realized that the conversation was going nowhere and motioned to Michael to bring him the phone.

Without saying another word he gave the phone to his dad and sat down on the couch next to him.

"Hello," said Michael's dad.

There was a pause in the conversation and then his dad said, with a kind of unusual look on his face, "That's not good."

At that point, Michael stood up and left the room.

Chapter 2

'THE BEGINNING of the nineteen eighties was like something out of a science fiction movie. There were all kinds of technology being developed and the computer was just beginning to catch on. Not too many people owned a personal computer or PC as they are called today. They soon became a common household appliance much like a microwave or TV. Today most people own PC's and use them in everyday life...'

"Why is this so boring?" Michael's thoughts crept out of his mouth.

"Ssshhh!" came from the mouth of the annoying girl who sat in front of him during his social studies class, and she was annoying in every sense of the word. Michael had even taken the time during a writing class to look up the word and write a description of her using the definition. He really disliked sitting in this desk with Molly, that was her name, so close to him.

She was tall, for a twelve year old, and she had the straightest, darkest brown hair he had ever seen. It was always in her face and on his desk, which really grossed him out.

He used to tell her, "If I want your hair on my desk I'll pull it out myself."

"This stuff is interesting isn't it?" Molly said with a smile that showed more metal than the front end of a '57 Buick. With her metal braces and wire rimmed glasses, Michael use to say she looked more like a hairy radio tower than a twelve year old girl.

Some of the students were reading their essay reports, that they had finished to the class.

"Leave me alone! If it is so interesting then turn around and pay attention," Michael snapped.

"Excuse me Michael, is there something you would like to add to our discussion?"

It was at that point Michael realized that his teacher, Mrs. Robinson, was talking to him. All he wanted to do was shove his pencil in his eye. "This is so frustrating," he said to himself.

"No, sorry I was just asking for a pencil so that I could take notes."

"Well do it quietly next time so you don't disrupt the class."

These were just the kind of things that made school seem to be the worst thing he could be doing right now, next to eating liver. It seemed that every time Molly annoyed him he was the one who got into trouble. His parents tried to tell him that it wasn't the one who started it, it's usually the one who responds that gets caught. This was more information he didn't think he would ever use or understand.

Just then his most favorite sound in the whole world entered his ear canal. That sound was the end of the school day. That loud, shrieking, ear piercing tone that meant it was time to go.

Michael sprang to his feet as if he was attached to a jack in the box. But before he could get very far, Mrs. Robinson reminded the class that their assignment the 'essay' was due tomorrow. That was very bad news for this young man, since he hadn't even started it yet. How did this week go by so fast? What was he going to do now? So close to happiness, and yet so far.

"When is dad coming home?" Michael grilled his mother. He was standing behind her while she worked on opening the mail.

"When does he always come home?" she replied.

"I don't have time to wait mom, I need help!" He said as he pointed to a notebook he had in his hand.

"If it has anything to do with math you're just going to have to wait, you know I can't do math above fourth grade."

"It's not math mom, I need to write a paper on some of the inventions of the nineteen hundreds and it is due tomorrow."

"Well then I suggest you get busy on it," his mother replied as she read through the mail.

"You don't understand," the whine began to enter his voice. He hated homework and this one was going to be the worst yet.

"What don't I understand?" His mother asked.

"I have to write a paper on inventions and I don't know how."

"How long does it need to be?" His mother questioned while turning to look at him.

"Ahhh…, at least ten pages."

"Why would your teacher give you a ten page assignment and make you have it done by tomorrow? Do I need to call her?" Michael's mother began to sound, lets just say, a bit annoyed.

Then it hit her. "You were waiting to the last minute again weren't you little boy?"

It seemed funny for her to call him that, since he was about the same height as her. But he also knew she was serious when she used that tone, and a feeling of depression came over him.

"It's not my fault," he said in his mind as he began to back up. He knew that if he said it out loud that he could get into some trouble, and he wanted to stay out of trouble this week so he could go to the party with his friends on Saturday.

"I tell you every day…, your father tells you every day…, don't wait until the last minute!" His mom began to lecture him.

Michael began to feel the hot jets of anger rush into his head. He hated it when he got lectured by his parents.

He just wanted some help with a paper, not a speech on how to be a good student. Why didn't his parents understand that he was not a good student and probably never would be?

As he turned to walk away he heard his mother speak, "Tell me what it is that you need to do and I will help you get started." She said this with that tone that he knew she used when she was just trying to get him going so he would leave her alone.

"I just have to write about some inventions, what they

were, and how they were important to the nineteen hundreds." He said in a way as if to minimize his problem.

"Well than just write about how the airplane changed the world, you know a lot about that."

"But mom…"

"Don't but mom, me!"

"Sorry…"

"Don't be sorry just get busy!"

At this point Michael knew it would be best to wait until his dad, who was now about a half of an hour late, to get home. He knew his dad would help him with the paper. His dad knew everything about anything. He could fly a plane, drive a truck, captain a boat, cook, clean… you get the picture.

"Mom, I'm hungry, where is dad?" questioned Michelle as she sat in front of the TV, her homework long since completed.

Michael's mother then realized that her husband was very late getting home from school. She knew he always got out a few minutes before her and sped home like there was no tomorrow. It was like some kind of race to see who could get home first.

Hmmm, she thought, I guess I should call him and find out where he is.

It was at that point they heard the door to the garage open and saw their dad come through it with a very concerned look on his face. He started to come in and tripped on the shoes sitting right in front of the door. He just pushed them out of the way and said, "Hi."

This came as a shock to the kids as well as their mother. Where was the yelling and complaining about the shoes? Why wasn't someone going to be punished?

Usually Michael would say something like. "Way to leave your shoes in the way Michelle!"

But the lack of anger from his dad had caught him by such a surprise that he said nothing and just went back to writing in his notebook.

His dad walked into the kitchen and right into an ambush of comments and questions he seemed to not want to answer.

"Where have you been…? I'm hungry… I need help… I need my diaper changed."

"Huh?"

It was little Kimberly standing there in a shirt covered with today's lunch, her cute little smile waiting for daddy to give her his hello kiss and hug.

"And how is my little Boo Bah doing today?" he asked her.

Seeing her seemed to make all the problems of daily life just fade away and he picked her up and gave her a huge kiss and hug.

"Dad I need help, you can play with her later!" Michael butted into the moment.

His dad set Kimberly down and turned to look at Michael.

"He has a paper due tomorrow that he hasn't started yet and it needs to be ten pages and he just has no…"

"Wait!" interrupted his dad to his mother's sentence.

"I need to talk to your mom first kids, so go play, when I'm done we'll eat, and then I will help you with whatever you need."

The kids turned to leave and Michael's foot got stuck in the chair near where he was standing and he fell to the floor. This brought a big laugh from his two sisters who, without him knowing it, had tied his shoe strings to the chair.

"That will teach you to wear your shoes in the house," his mother said while laughing at his situation.

"I needed that like I needed an extra pimple on my nose," Michael said to himself as he untied his shoes from the chair. He turned to look angrily at his two sisters as they turned and ran from the room. He dragged himself up off of the floor and left the room to start his paper. He wasn't sure how, but he knew he needed to get it done. He couldn't take another bad grade. He would have to put off getting back at his sisters until later.

His parents had told him, "One more 'F' and it's off to private school for you."

Like that would matter. Didn't they understand, it wasn't the school that he hated it was going to school, any school!

He sat in a chair and stared at the blank page wondering how to begin. He could hear his parents talking in the kitchen. He couldn't quite make out what they were saying because they were talking so low. It was the kind of talk they would have when it concerned him and his work in school. But this time it was different and he knew it was not about him.

A few moments passed and his dad walked into the room. He sat down next to Michael and asked, "How is it going?"

At first Michael wasn't sure how to answer. I mean his only answer could have been: "It's not going."

"I have no idea where to begin, and I'm not sure what to write about."

"Your mom said she suggested you write about the airplane and how it changed the world."

"Yeah, and I'm trying to figure out where to start."

"I'll tell you what, start with the Wright Brothers and end with the B-2 Bomber and fill in the rest with anything you can remember from what I have told you about."

That was his dad's way of solving his problem, by making it sound so easy.

He didn't want to admit he really never paid any attention to his dad when he talked about flying and the history of flying. He knew his dad was a pilot in the Air Force before he became a teacher, and he knew his dad still flew planes in the Air Force Reserve, he was reminded of that on the way home from school the other day, but he knew little else.

"Why can't I just use the computer and get the information off of the internet?" Michael questioned his dad as he stood up.

"Is that what you are suppose to do, or are you just looking for a quick way out of this?" His dad said as he turned back toward Michael.

"I can use the internet, but I have to put it in my own words."

"Well then go ahead and get started, I'm going to make dinner before your sister starves, so get busy and after dinner I'll help you if I can."

That one sentence about his sister brought a smile to Michael's face. He always was on her case about eating.

"She only wears a watch so she knows when it's time for breakfast, lunch, and dinner," he always joked.

His dad walked away and Michael went to the computer room to see if he could get on the internet to start his paper.

Chapter 3

THE SUN came through his window like a bolt of lightning on a hot summer night. He groaned and knew that a new day had dawned and it was time to face the music... His paper wasn't completed.

"Where did this week go?" Once again raced through his mind.

The big question he knew he would hear this morning from his parents was... "Is your paper finished?"

He wrote most of it last night, way into the late hours. He had gotten enough information off of the internet, with the help of his parents, to get a good start. It must have been well after eleven when he made it to bed. Tired and rundown from all the work, he hit the bed and fell right to sleep.

His dad helped with some suggestions and some facts, but seemed to be preoccupied with something else the entire time. Michael never seemed to find a time or words to ask what was going on, so he just let it go. Then with sleep, his mind seemed to be erased of all events of the day.

"Let's go!" came a holler from downstairs.

"You're going to be late if you don't get up!"

He threw the covers back and started to sit up when he got a pain in his back.

"Ouch!"

"What the… what is this?"

Michael pulled a small Lego toy out from under him. He had been sleeping on it all night and only now felt the pain of it. At the same time he was discovering this discomforting bed bug, his little sister Kimberly entered his room.

"That for you," she said in the soft voice of a three year old, pointing at the toy.

"Thanks, I needed this," Michael replied.

She went over to him and gave him a hug.

"Good morning Mikey." She had called him that since she could speak and he really didn't mind.

"Good morning Kimberly," he replied in a half asleep voice.

She turned and left his room as if she was only there to make sure he was awake. He continued to struggle with the morning and eventually managed to get out of his bed. Michael loved to sleep and really hated to get up in the morning.

"Wow! I need a nap," he said out loud to himself.

The only thing that made it easier for Michael to get out of the bed and start his day was that he knew it was Friday. This meant a weekend of no school and sleeping in. Just get through the day and you have two free ones, he thought.

He dressed quickly, with just a pair of shorts and a t-shirt, and he made it downstairs, ready for school in record time.

"Are you finished with your paper?" his mom inquired.

"I'm not sure."

"Just let it go," his dad said looking at his mom. His dad knew it wasn't finished and he didn't want to listen to him argue with his mother about it.

"I'm sure he can work on it in school and get it done by the end of the day. We need to get going so we're not late." His dad was always so punctual.

"Yeah, I can do that," Michael said nodding his head toward his dad.

His dad was looking at a newspaper on the counter, trying to show his mother something, and seemed to be in a hurry.

The rest of the morning was uneventful and Michael made it to school just as the bell rang. He was sitting in his first period class daydreaming, as usual, when it dawned on him that he hadn't combed his hair. Usually he just combed it flat and let it hang on his forehead. But this morning, for some reason, he had completely forgotten to do this.

It really didn't matter what his hair looked like. It seems that these days any style worked. He had seen kids in school with hair that looked as if it had never been combed, so he just didn't care about it. Why should he, with all of the wild hair styles. But, it did make him wonder where his mind had been.

"Nice hair," his friend Matthew said rubbing his hand over his head.

"Thanks, I thought I would try something different today. You know me, always living on the edge."

Matthew jumped over the chair and sat down, and turned to look at Michael.

"Are you going to Tyler's party on Saturday?"

"Yea, are you?" Michael said in response to Matthew's question.

"I hope so, but my mom is a little mad at me about my grades."

"Seems to be going around." Michael said with a sigh.

"Did you finish your paper for last period?" Matthew said turning back to the front as the teacher walked into the room.

"No, but I will." Michael's voice trailed off.

He quickly returned to his daydream, except it wasn't a dream. He was realizing that his dad still had the real serious look about things this morning. Not the usual worried look that he would get when he was paying bills or going over his school work. No, this was different, and as far as he could tell it started last Saturday, with the phone call.

Yes, it was all coming together now, the late arrival from work, the phone call, the conversation with his mom, the lack of attention to things going on. "But what is going on?" he wondered in his mind.

"Hey, let's go!" Matthew interrupted Michael's thoughts.

"Class is over dude, get up."

"What did we do today?"

"Are you kidding me? You missed the whole class and you weren't absent?"

"There is a brain teaser for you," he thought. "I was actually in a class and can't remember what it was about. I really need to work on this problem." He stood up and headed into the hall, where his problem got worse, because coming down the hall, right toward him, with a very serious look on her face was Molly.

"I Iide me!" Michael said to Matthew.

21

"No way, I'm not talking to her!" Matthew said as he took off down the hall towards the gym.

"Do you realize I spent five hours last night typing this paper for you?" She yelled in one of her most annoying voices. "I have been looking all over for you, where have you been?"

Molly then pulled a paper from her folder, it was an essay and it had Michael's name on it.

"I was just out helping the janitor clean up the parking lot, where do you think I've been?" Michael responded.

Well that's it, his problem is solved. Molly had typed a ten page paper on inventions of the nineteen hundreds and it was Michael's. What else could he ask for? He lived a charmed life.

But his problem wasn't solved. He had been brought up to tell the truth, to be honest with everything he did. To this point, that is what he had done. He never lied to anyone at school, not the teachers or his parents. He had found out a long time ago it was easier to tell the truth than to lie and get caught. He also had never taken anything that didn't belong to him. But this, this would get him out of trouble and he wouldn't have to do the work. Then a little voice in his mind said, 'what will you do when your parents find out?'

"I can't use this," he said in a sort of disgusted voice as she handed him the paper. He handed it back and turned to walk away.

"What's wrong with you Michael Rossi?"

"Nothing is wrong with me, I just don't take credit for things that I didn't do."

"I did this for you because I wanted to help."

"That's fine and I appreciate it, but I must do my own

work, and fail myself without anyone's help." He turned and began to follow Matthew toward the gym.

He couldn't help but wonder what she was after. It wasn't everyday she helped him, usually it was the opposite. As a matter of fact, all that she had done lately was to get him in trouble.

He paused for a minute, shook his head clear, and walked off. His favorite subject was about to begin and he didn't want to be late.

Molly stood there for a moment and couldn't figure out what had gone wrong. She thought she was doing a favor for him and instead she ended up wasting five hours of her time. "Oh well," she thought, "It's his loss."

PE had ended and it was time for his next class. He realized he must focus to finish the work he was behind on before the end of the day. He spent all of Math class and most of lunch writing. A couple of times he was interrupted by his teachers asking questions. But he was able to continue working on his paper and by the time his class with Mrs. Robinson came around he had finished enough to at least get a passing grade.

There was no one as happy as he was when the dismissal bell rang and he turned in his paper. He let out a big smile as he laid it on the teacher's desk, grinning at the surprised look in her eyes. He was also very happy that he didn't have to read it to the class. He knew his teacher couldn't believe he could finish this paper on time. He hadn't finished one on time yet and he knew she was shocked by the look on her face.

"I hope this is your own work young man," she said with a stern look on her face.

He wanted to say, "Nope, I found it on my way to school and thought I would just use it," but he knew that would be disrespectful and not acceptable to his parents, or anyone else for that matter, so he just smiled and left quietly.

On the walk home he couldn't help but think how ironic it was to be accused of not doing his own work when he could have very easily taken the paper from Molly.

"Is this what the world is all about? What happened to common courtesy?" He said aloud.

"What are you talking about?" Matthew said as he came up behind Michael and tried to trip him.

"Oh, never mind."

"Let's just get home and start this much needed weekend with no homework!"

Michael kicked off his shoes, dropped his book bag, and was on the couch in three large leaps. He lay sprawled out like a dead tuna at the fish market. His mind was overwhelmed with the events of the week. All the school work, all of the homework, the mysterious problem his dad seemed to be having, and he was tired.

He turned on the TV and began to flip through the channels looking for something to watch.

His mind began to settle down and it was as if it was saying to him, "There are times when a child just needs to relax, and this is one of them."

He would tell his parents when he was in grade school, so many years ago, that school caused him to have brain damage. His dad had a list of unexplained events in his life that might support his theory, but he could also point out school was not the cause of these momentary lapses of reason that he had.

Nevertheless, he was exhausted. A good afternoon nap would be just the thing he needed to recharge the old batteries for an event filled weekend. He drifted off to sleep as the sound of the TV played in his ears.

"I'm flying, I'm really flying and I don't have wings...!"

"Hey, get up, and stop drooling on my couch pillow!"

Michael's eyes opened and he saw his dad turn to walk back into the kitchen. He looked down and saw the puddle of water on the pillow where his head had crashed down when he hit the couch.

"I must have been dreaming," he thought in his mind. What a dream he had. He was actually flying like a bird over his house and he was looking down at his family who couldn't believe what they were seeing.

"How was school today, Bud?"

His dad had a lot of nicknames for the kids and one of the most common for him was "Bud." He wasn't sure how it came to be. He knew of an adult drink with that name, but didn't think he was named after it.

"It was fine. I turned in my paper and we had PE today."

"You did? You turned in your paper? Was it done? Did you do it yourself?"

Each time he tried to answer his dad had another question. Why is everyone so surprised that he finished a paper?

"I did it in school just like you said I would."

"Can I go to play with my friends?" he quickly added so he could avoid any further interrogations.

"Do you have any homework tonight?" his dad asked.

25

Michael said, "No, it's Friday." In his mind he was thinking, "Are you new here?"

"Yeah, go ahead, but when you see your mom, I want you to come home."

Michael would usually try to negotiate a time to come home, but this time for some reason he could not explain, he just said okay, and stepped out the door.

There are several people who can tell you that he would make either a good lawyer or a politician because of his ability to negotiate. He could argue about anything, just to try and get his way. Sometimes it worked, and sometimes it didn't. He figured it just depended on the person, the subject, and what type of mood his mom and dad were in.

As he walked through the garage to go out into the yard he noticed that in the back of his dad's truck was his military flight bag. He only had it when he was going to do his weekends in the reserve. He thought that it was strange to see it today, since his dad had not been scheduled to fly this weekend, and he had said nothing about leaving this weekend.

He paused in the garage for a moment and thought, 'strange…, what is going on?'

But like any other child with a short attention span, he turned and went into the front yard to look for something to do. He took in a breath of fresh air and cleared his mind. A feeling of relief had come over him and he was happy to be out of school for the weekend.

"Maybe we will get a snow storm before Monday," he said in a low voice. This, he knew, was not likely since it was only mid October. In this part of the country that just didn't happen. He could still feel the warm air of early fall and the sun was bright and warm in the late afternoon. It almost felt as if summer were still going on, but the signs told him differently. It was a sea of color. Each tree seemed to burst into a fire of fall colors. The reds and oranges were so bright and clear. There was a flock of geese in the familiar V formation honking overhead. The grass was green and had that sweet smell of fall to it. He liked the smell of fresh cut grass in the fall. It made him want to lay in it and just enjoy the afternoon.

As he gazed back up the street in the direction that his mother would be coming in, he saw his friend Adam, so he decided to go over and see what was going on with him.

He trotted up the street towards his friend. He would have ridden his bike, but he had a flat and didn't have time to fix it. Or was it that he was just too busy with other things to worry about a flat tire on his bike?

Either way, he knew he would get it fixed. It was like everything else to him, once he found the time he could do just about anything. That was one of the special powers he always knew he had. He could take apart and fix just about anything. One time he took apart his sister's bike just for fun. He later found out it really wasn't that much fun when his sister told on him. That was definitely one of those things he would have been better off thinking about before doing. Still, he had fun doing it and it was no big deal for him to put it back together. He just made it seem like he didn't know how to annoy his sister a little more.

He had reached the top of the street where Adam was and he started to tell him about school and what Molly had done, but before he could get too far with it he saw his mother coming home with his two sisters.

"Oh, I need to go," he said as he began to run down the street toward his home.

On occasion he would be in the street when one of his parents came home and he liked to race them into the driveway. Michael was very fast, he claimed to be one of the fastest in his class. All his parents knew was that he was able to outrun them at times. He was reaching top speed in only a few steps and his breathing was steady as his long legs churned under him. It wasn't all that difficult to win, his mom had to stop at an intersection in the neighborhood that had a stop sign. This gave Michael a little advantage since he could just run through it on the sidewalk.

They all arrived in the garage at about the same time and Michael opened his mom's door.

"Ha, I win again!"

"Yeah you did, but I'll get you one of these days," his mom quipped back.

"Get your sister out of her seat," requested his mother.

Kimberly, being only three, was still in a car seat, and Michael knew that was a good idea since she was just a little midget. Not a real midget, just very small for her age. Actually, Kimberly was a lot like a little doll to the family. She was a very petite and proper little girl. Her parents where just amazed at how polite she was at such a young age. They would compare her quite often to how impolite Michael was at the same age, and they had many videos to prove it. Videos that they used to bring out just to show him how he had fought with his sister since they were both in diapers.

He opened the door to the side Kimberly was on and she yelled, "Hi Mikey! I go potty today!"

He said, "Hi, me too," and then proceeded to remove her from her seat.

While he was doing this he told his mother about how

he finished his assignment and turned it in on time. She was a little surprised, as most seemed to be, but gave him a big smile and a "Good Job!"

Then as a group, Michael, his mom, and both sisters, entered the house talking and laughing. It was nice to be home on a Friday and they really enjoyed finishing another week of school.

As they cleared the entry and spread out into the house Michael could see his dad talking on the phone.

"Who is he talking too?" asked his mom.

"I don't know, I was outside," replied Michael.

Here was the second time his dad was having what looked like a very serious phone call, and Michael then remembered about the flight bag in the truck.

"Is dad going away this weekend?"

"Not as far as I know," Michael's mother said with a sort of confused look.

Just as she said that his dad said "Goodbye" and hung up the phone.

"I need to see all of you, come in here," his dad commanded from the front room.

Michael looked at his mother and could see she was a bit concerned, or annoyed, sometimes it was hard to tell the difference. He had no idea what could be going on, but he knew family meetings were rare, and especially on a Friday night.

Chapter 4

MICHAEL CAN remember many things about growing up. He had been to many different places and experienced many different things. You can say he had seen and done a lot for an eleven year old. His favorite place to visit besides grandma's house was Disneyland. He loved it there! His favorite ride was the big roller coaster he went on with his mother. He would hang on to her and scream and as soon as they got off, he wanted to go again.

He also loved going to the beach. It was so fun to go into the waves and body surf. He liked to track down the marine life at night on the beach. In all of the things he had done and all of the places he had gone, he had always been with his family, and now he had an uneasy feeling as he sat down on a chair in the room with his mom, dad, and two sisters. What possibly could be so important as to interrupt his weekend of peace and relaxation?

Michael's dad stood by the window, partially hidden in the glare coming through it. He squinted a bit to see his father's face. His dad moved and the glare was gone and he had a kind of inquisitive look on his face as he looked at Michael.

"What's wrong with your face?"

Michael was still sitting in the chair with his face all squinted up, trying to see through the glare. The only thing was there was no more glare because his dad had moved. His face was just behind in getting back to normal.

"Nothing, I was just…"

"Never mind that, just pay attention!" His father's voice was becoming rather serious.

Michael's dad wasn't a large man, actually, he was about average size for an adult of his age, which Michael thought was old. But he did have a certain way of being intimidating and he commanded respect from his children.

Michael was like most adolescents under the age of twenty, anyone over forty was considered to be a senior citizen. He thought his grandparents were really old, and his great-grandma must have seen the pilgrims land at Plymouth.

His parents had met around twenty years ago. He wasn't sure but thought he remembered hearing that number recently. They actually had been married for about eighteen years. Most of Michael's friends' parents had been divorced, so he felt pretty lucky to have what he did. He would listen to his friends tell him who they were going to be with and on what weekend, and Michael would just think how lucky he was not to have to do those things. He loved his parents very much and couldn't bear the thought of them not being together.

But this was not what the conversation was to be about. Actually, he never thought the problem was with his parents. He had a feeling that it had something to do with his dad's job in the military.

Michael's dad was a pilot and had been a pilot for a long time. That was how he had met Michael's mother. They told him a story of how they met at an airbase one Sunday afternoon during an air show. His dad's story always differed from his mother's. According to his dad, his mother was hooked the minute they made eye contact, his mother claimed his dad was. He really didn't care, he just knew that without them he wouldn't be here right now.

His dad used to leave a lot when Michael was young. He was always going to some kind of a war game or something. He had only seen pictures of his dad in his plane and once his dad showed him a video of his plane bombing a target on a range. It was cool to see the bomb explode and destroy the target.

He didn't really have too much information about his dad during those days since he really didn't talk about it much. His mother told him once that his dad was in a war somewhere near a gulf and that he didn't like to talk about it since he had lost one of his best friends there. Michael didn't really remember any of this because he was too small at the time, and his dad had gotten out of the Air Force when he was only four. But he did remain in the reserves, which Michael only knew as a weekend job.

That was one reason why they had moved to their new home. His dad wanted to fly some other type of plane and he could only do that where they were now.

His family's history really wasn't that important to him at this stage of his life. He knew his father's family was from Italy because he always ate at an Italian restaurant one of his relatives owned near his grandparents. The pictures on the wall were of his ancestors in Italy. Of course, with a last name like Rossi, what else could he be?

The only thing he knew about his mother's family was that they all lived very far away. He wouldn't see them very often, but did enjoy it when his other grandmother would visit from Nevada.

His mother sat on a chair on the other side of the room. Her legs were crossed and her hands were in her lap. He loved his mom, she was so beautiful. She had long brown hair that she liked to wear in a pony tail. Her fingernails were always done with some crazy color and design.

She loved to be different. When they had first moved into their new house, she painted half of the basement a really bright tangerine color and when she was finished she announced to the children, "Stay out of my side of the room!" motioning with her hands in a circular movement.

She had a lot of craft things that he wasn't allowed to touch, but on occasion she would let him paint a few things. He liked that, it went to his creative side.

When they would go places she would always buy him stuff. It was as if she was into the same things he was. She liked to look at the toys and all of the new action figures.

The one thing he didn't like was when she would try to hold his hand in public. He thought he was getting too old for that. She would soon point out though that he was still her little boy.

She smiled at him, the smile of a warm, loving mother. He always liked it when she did that because it meant he was not in trouble. He was her only son and used that to his advantage. Every time he would do something to annoy her he would point out that he was her only son. She would always joke with him about how much trouble he was at birth. "And how that had continued for eleven years." But it was easy to see how much she really loved him.

As they looked across the room at each other she winked at Michael and smiled. He knew right then that whatever this was about, it was going to be all right.

His dad began to speak about the university where he worked and something about an experiment that he was starting.

"What is he talking about?" Michael's mind began to wander. As usual, he once again wasn't paying attention. His dad noticed that immediately and motioned with his two fingers to Michael's eyes and back to his and said, "Look at me and listen!"

He realized instantly that this was serious and he should get his mind off of being a cartoon character in bikini bottom and on to the conversation at hand.

"I'm listening….!" he said with a sense of urgency.

"Right?" his sister Michelle butted into his sentence.

"Hey! Knock it off!" came from across the room where his mom sat. "Pay attention, this is important!"

As Michael's gaze reached back to his dad he noticed a kind of puzzled look on his face, and then his face became serious again. "This isn't good…" raced through his mind. Michael sat up and gave his undivided attention to his dad.

"I don't know if you guys have noticed lately, but I have had some things on my mind."

The only thing Michael had on his mind was the word, "Duh."

Had he been that unaware that his family, especially Michael, was stressed over his unusual behavior for the last few days?

His dad went on to explain about a project he was working on at the college where he was a professor. The project was about people living in an extreme environment for an extended period of time. His dad had a degree in science and flight. How did he end up working in an area of what seemed to be sociology? "See I did learn something in school," he thought in his mind. A small smile came across his face.

His dad continued to tell them about some of the problems he was having with a decision that involved them somehow. He was talking about leaving for several weeks and he wanted their opinion. He had also mentioned something about not flying fighter planes anymore. He said he was now going to be in a unit with cargo planes. This was all of no interest to Michael.

His mother was questioning why they were discussing that now. "If you're still working on this why do we need to know now?" She asked.

His dad looked at her with a strange look and then continued. "I called this meeting because I wanted to know where you wanted to eat tonight."

"That's it, that's the big meeting? What about all this stuff going on, what about the phone calls, and the bag, and the crazy mood?" Michael's head was all a blur with questions to himself.

Could he have made all of this stuff up in his head? He did have a really crazy imagination. But the events of the past week were real. There was no way he could have made all of that up.

His mom said, "Mexican," stood up and started for the door.

Michelle and Kimberly were right on her heels as they

35

put on their shoes and headed for the garage. Michael's dad already had on shoes and was getting his keys when he noticed Michael was still sitting on the chair looking a bit confused.

"Let's go Bud…, aren't you hungry?" His dad said as he walked back toward him.

"I thought you had something important to say, and all you wanted to know was where we wanted to eat?"

"Look, sometimes life can be really stressful," his dad began in a low voice.

"I have a lot on my mind right now and I thought it would be nice to go and eat as a family and just forget about the week."

"My thoughts exactly!" screamed through Michael's mind.

"Alright, so let's go!"

They headed out into the garage to join the rest of the family for a night out on the town.

On the way to the restaurant Michael was listening to his dad explain to his mom that he had been offered a chance to go to some laboratory and do some research. He didn't know what it was all about, but he listened intently trying to get as much information as he could.

"I would leave in February and return sometime in March or April," he said as he navigated his way through the never ending line of Friday evening traffic.

His mom was not impressed with this. She kept saying, "No way can you be gone that long without us. Find someone else, you can't be doing this!"

It seemed as though his dad was agreeing with her. Like it wasn't his idea and he had no choice.

He worked his way into the restaurant parking lot and turned to look at his wife. In a soft voice, trying to not let the children hear, he said, "We can finish this later."

"Why do we always have to eat at a Mexican restaurant? Why can't we just go to McDonalds?" Michael's words were lost in the noisy parking lot as his family headed toward the door.

"Did you say something Michael?" his dad inquired.

"No, I was just talking to myself."

"Well stop it before people think you're crazy or something."

Why would someone think he was crazy for talking to himself? Most of the time he was the only one listening anyway. But, he just followed along into the restaurant. For some reason as they entered, for some reason that he couldn't explain, he asked his dad if he could go with him on his job to that laboratory he was talking about.

Chapter 5

"FINALLY, IT'S Saturday and I can go to Tyler's party! I have been waiting for this for weeks and now it's finally here!" Michael's mind was all a blur with his excitement.

"Tyler has the best parties! He has a really cool Xbox, and his yard is really huge!" Michael would tell his parents after visiting there the first time last year, after he had first met him in school.

Today was his birthday and Tyler had bragged at school for weeks about how much fun they were going to have. He had invited all of Michael's friends and they were sure to have a good time talking about video games, bugs, and not school.

He hopped down the steps and into the normal Saturday household. His sisters were on the couch watching TV, Dora or Sponge Bob…, his mother was at the table drinking coffee and pouring over the newspaper…, and dad…

"Where's dad?"

"He had to go to work today," she said this between sips of coffee.

"Glad I'm not him," Michael thought. "It should be against the law to have to go to school on a Saturday."

"I am going to get ready for the party," he said as he looked at the digital clock on the microwave above the stove.

It was already almost ten and the party started at noon. Michael turned and ran back up the steps to his room to get dressed.

He could hear his mother yell as he made it to the top of the steps, "Make sure that room is clean before you go!"

It was always something. Being a kid today was so difficult. Clean your room, wash you hands, do your homework…, so much to do and so little time.

But he did it anyway, he cleaned up his room and fixed his bed. His mind was on how much fun he was going to have today. He dressed and combed his hair. The last thing he did was run down the steps and yell, "I'm going mom!" And then he ran out of the front door.

"You be careful, have fun, and don't forget to be home by six!" his mother yelled from the kitchen.

Six o'clock came and went and Michael was nowhere to be seen. His mother and father weren't worried about him though. They knew he was only a few houses away and they had the phone number to where he was if they really needed to get him.

Shortly after six-fifteen he came strolling in the front door looking exhausted from a long day of running and partying.

"How was it?" A voice from the couch said as he entered the house.

"It was good we had so much fun and he got some cool

stuff!" Michael's words soared into the room where his dad lay on the couch looking just as exhausted as Michael was.

"Hey, did your mom tell you the news this morning?"

Michael had no idea what his dad was talking about. All he could remember from this morning was getting ready to leave and then leaving. In his excitement he had completely forgotten that his dad wasn't even home. The last thing he remembered was saying goodbye.

"No." He said as he went into the kitchen to get a drink.

"That job I told you about last night, the one where I have to leave and set up a laboratory for the university, I might get to take all of you with me!" His dad began to explain as he stood up to go into the kitchen with Michael.

"I am going to be flying to a remote location inside the Artic Circle with supplies to set up a laboratory for studying our atmosphere and how global warming is…"

Michael had a very confused look on his face. He could see his dad's lips moving, he could hear the word's coming out of his mouth, but he had no idea what he was saying.

"And I might be able to take you with me if you want to go." His dad ended the sentence and then stood waiting for a reply from his son.

Silence…

"Well?"

"Does this mean I can get out of school?" Was about all he could think to say.

That night, all through dinner, after dinner, and into the

late evening hours, Michael's dad explained about what he was going to do and the part his family had in it.

His job was going to be to fly in the cargo and oversee the construction of a laboratory and living quarters for up to twenty people.

They were then going to be flying people up to a remote location inside the Artic Circle. This meant it would be a very cold and dark place.

The university his dad worked for was given a grant from the U.S. Government to study the upper atmosphere over the North Pole to determine the effects of global warming.

Michael had totally missed that part earlier when his dad had the family meeting on Friday. He thought it was all about people living together in a harsh environment, like he saw on reality TV. But this was different it was about science and studying our world. An adventure…?

"That wasn't too bad at all," he thought to himself as he listened to his dad go over some of the details of what he was going to be doing.

"Before we actually get the place up and running I am going to have to be there for an extended period of time. I have the permission of my supervisors to take you with me if you would like to go." His dad continued to explain.

"What about school…, what about my friends…, what about where it's located?!" Were just some of the questions being asked by the family.

Each time Michael could think of a question someone else had already asked it. His mother had the most questions, being she was not too thrilled about moving an entire family to an isolated place with no stores or doctors… etc.

41

His dad was doing his best to answer the questions one at a time and before long it was getting late and time for bed. This was good because Michael was very tired from a long day of partying, but he was also becoming very interested in what his dad was saying. Being the adventurer that he was, this sounded like something right up his alley.

"Let's call it a night and we can continue this conversation tomorrow. We have some time before it all starts and we can get all of our questions answered before we make a decision." His dad ended the discussion and directed the kids to bed.

Kimberly was already asleep in her mother's arms and Michelle's eyes were getting heavy. Michael was a little bit jazzed about the prospect of exploring the North Pole, but he realized sleep was near and so with the others, he headed up to bed. The thoughts of snow, ice, and maybe the chance to see where Santa lived, were on his mind as he closed his eyes and fell asleep.

Sunday morning came, and Michael arose to the sound, and smell of breakfast being cooked. He stumbled down the steps and into the kitchen. Everyone was already up and eating. "Wow, is it already ten?" Michael seemed to be unaware that he had slept so late today. Not that this was unusual. He liked to sleep in, especially on the weekends, but for some reason he felt like today he should have been up earlier.

His dad had made him some bacon, his favorite, and eggs. He loved breakfast on Sunday's, this was usually the only time he got to eat bacon, except for the times when his parents would buy him a bacon cheeseburger at his favorite fast food establishment.

As he ate, he began to question his dad some more about what he had told them last night.

"When do we get to go to that place, dad?" Michael inquired as he shoved his breakfast in his mouth.

"Well," his dad began.

"I have to get the first people up there before December and get the buildings in place. We can't wait until after that because of the weather problems that happen up there in the winter. Next we will begin to put in the computers and supplies for the scientists who will be living there. That is when we come in, probably in spring we can get going."

"In the spring? Why do we have to wait so long?" Michael began to reach the point of complaining.

"That's just the way it is, be patient." His dad said with a rather stern voice.

Michael's mother was listening to all of this and seemed to be a bit uninterested in when they went. She still wasn't sure this was such a good idea.

"We really haven't said we were going for sure yet," she added.

Michael began to think as he tuned out his parent's conversation. It was only about a month and a half to December and then three more months to spring time. Heck, he could wait four or five months.

"Wait a minute, that means I will have to continue with school and homework and that is just not acceptable!" He thought to himself as he finished his breakfast.

Chapter 6

As THE days passed, things kind of returned to normal around the house. It was get up in the morning, go to school, come home from school, do homework, eat and back to bed. It was kind of a boring routine and it seemed like it took forever for the weeks to pass.

But they did and before he knew it, November had arrived. His dad had been back and forth a few times to the location. Each time he was gone about four days. When he got back he would just say how things were going and that they were ahead of schedule. That was good news to Michael, he hoped that maybe they could get going earlier than expected.

Michael's mother however, did not share his enthusiasm for the earlier schedule. She wanted to have Thanksgiving and Christmas at their house and not in the middle of nowhere.

His dad had assured her they would not be going until after the holidays. That seemed to be okay with Michael, Christmas and New Year's were his favorite holidays next to Halloween, his birthday, and that had already passed. He had celebrated his twelfth birthday party with some friends. He loved it because after the party they had all gone trick or treating together.

"We need to do some training before we go," his dad said one night during a conversation.

This brought a little bit of an argument from the members of the family. The main question being, "What training?"

"What, did you think we were just going on vacation or something?"

"Yes!" the entire family said in unison.

"It won't be so bad, you just have to get fitted for your winter gear and then learn a little bit about survival in the winter."

"I already know about that, I do it every year." Michael said with the confidence of a bus driver talking about how to get around town.

"Oh, my boy, you are so misled," his dad added looking at Michael with a sort of pitiful face.

"Well, how bad could it be?" Michael continued with a shrug of his shoulders.

"It was forty-five degrees below zero last week and that was at the beginning of winter."

Michael's mother shivered and made the brrrr sound. "That's cold!" she added.

"The wind chill, which is the wind speed added to the air temperature, was even colder than that." His dad continued to give the weather report for the place they would be going. This was not intimidating to Michael, he was used to extremes. Remember, he had homework every night and lived with two sisters.

For the next couple of weeks leading up to Thanksgiving, Michael's family would watch DVD's on survival and practice some techniques that they were taught. His dad was explaining the whole trip part by part, while his family was making the necessary arrangements to be gone for a couple of weeks. This along with his school work was taking up most of his time. But that was okay with him since he wouldn't have school once he got to the Arctic.

It was at the end of that thought one evening, as if on queue, his dad announced to the children, "Your mother is going because she is going to be your teacher."

"Oh no, the worst thing that could ever have happened has. I'm going to be in my mom's class!" Michael gasped. His brain was having a hard time wrapping around that thought. The only thing he could think of in that moment is, "I'm not going!"

But instead, out of his mouth came the words, "Dad, why?"

His mother looked rather surprised. "What? You don't want me to be your teacher and kiss you every day in front of the class?"

"Mom!" Michael began in a panicked voice.

"Who else is going to be in this 'class'?" He made the quotation mark symbols with his fingers.

Michael's dad interrupted the exchange to further explain.

"We are going to be joined by three other families. They are all part of the company that is working on this station and they all have school aged children."

Michael and Michelle sat down to listen.

"Do you kids remember back in October when I was kind of preoccupied with phone calls and work?"

"Yea, I think so," answered Michael as if he had just met his dad for the first time.

"I was trying to get permission for your mom to go with me and be the teacher at the site. My boss wasn't going to allow it, but I was able to convince him, and that is how all of you are able to go with me."

Michael's mother had kind of a half smile on her face as he looked at her. Michael was always sure that his mother was not really thrilled about the prospect of spending a few weeks at a complex inside the Artic Circle. But she was an adventurous person, just like Michael, and she had agreed.

The most fun for everyone came on the day they were to be fitted for their winter survival gear. This was a one-piece suit and some gloves to most people. But to Michael's dad it was their "Winter Survival Gear" or 'WSG'.

They went to an airbase just outside of Washington, DC. Michael recognized it as the place his dad would go to fly on weekends, actually it was Andrews Air Force Base. "The place where the President has his plane." His dad had explained to them.

It was fun for the kids because they got to put on these really nice, heavy, warm suits and then run around in a simulated winter environment.

"This is so cool!" Michael screamed as he ran around in the fake snow and ice.

Michelle was also having a blast rolling in the snow and sliding down the little hills that were in the simulator. Kimberly looked like a little teddy bear of some sort and she was having some trouble keeping her balance under the weight of the suit. She kept falling over and she couldn't get up. Michael thought this was hilarious and even started to knock her down so he could laugh some more. This brought the "look" from his mother and he immediately stopped.

All the way home the kids laughed and joked about the fun they had and kept saying to their parents, "I can't wait to go!"

"First things first," their dad responded.

"We need to make some last minute arrangements and then enjoy our holidays before we go."

For Thanksgiving, they traveled to Michael's grandparent's house for their traditional dinner.

His grandparent's lived in Ohio and it was about a six hour drive. He didn't mind it to much because it gave him a chance to catch up on some sleep.

For Thanksgiving dinner, they ate salad, turkey, stuffing, potatoes, gravy, corn, a huge lasagna, and for dessert, pies… lots of pies.

Michael had reached his puberty stage, he was now twelve, and seemed to be in a growth spurt because he ate and ate, and when he was finished, he ate some more. It was all so good to him he couldn't help it.

His mother said at one point, "Take it easy or you will need to be refitted for your suit."

He just laughed. He did look like he had swallowed a basketball though, his stomach was stuck out from all of the food he had eaten.

All of his relatives were there, his aunts and uncles and even his great grandma, who was always smiling at the children and wanting hugs. Michael loved his family very much and really enjoyed being able to be together with all of them to celebrate the holiday.

After dinner he sat on the couch with his grandpa, dad, and some of his uncles, as they watched a football game. That seemed to be a tradition, eat and watch football. He really didn't follow too much football, being that most of it was on Sunday, his outside play day. He did like to sit and watch it with his dad and grandpa though, because he liked to hear them complain about the players and how 'dumb' a play might be. He also liked how they would complain about eating too much and then go right back in the kitchen for some pie and coffee. It was funny to Michael, he joked a lot about how he was like his grandfather, the 'Human Garbage Can'.

Michael needed a little break after such a big meal. He knew that soon he would get to jump into the leftovers, turkey sandwiches with mayonnaise. He loved to eat those on toast and he was sure his grandma would help him fix one as soon as he was hungry again.

Later in the day, his aunts and uncles left to go home and Michael got a big kiss and hug from each of them. They also wished him luck on his trip to the Arctic.

As every good day goes this one went by way too fast. It seemed like before anyone could even digest their dinner it was already Sunday and time to return home to Virginia, another six hour drive and another six hour nap.

The three weeks prior to the Christmas break went by rather fast for everyone. There was so much to do and prepare for this trip. Michael did not realize everything that needed to be done just to go north for a few weeks.

Before he knew it he was laying down to sleep on Christmas Eve. He loved this night, how peaceful it seemed. His dad always cooked a traditional Italian dinner on Christmas

Eve, with the seven kinds of fish, which only his dad would eat. The rest of the family had macaroni and cheese and ravioli's. They would then go to church, and it was always so beautiful with the lights and people singing. They would return home and change into their pajamas and then start nagging their parents to let them open a gift. Their mother was okay with it, but their dad was more of a traditionalist and wanted them to wait until morning.

As he lay there this Christmas Eve, he was looking out his window as it began to snow. This was the first time in his life that it was snowing on Christmas Eve and it made him feel kind of nice. He jumped out of bed to get a better look. It was so beautiful, there were large flakes that stuck to everything. They were reflecting in the lights on the house and throughout the neighborhood.

"Wow," he said softly to himself. "This is incredible, the stuff I only would see in movies."

He just stood there staring out at the beautiful scene. It made him feel kind of funny inside. Sort of a feeling he didn't understand. He started to think about some of the gifts that he had gotten throughout the years. He remembered back when he was around five or six and he got his first large ship made of Lego's. He remembered how his dad and grandfather worked on it all day and into the night to put it together for him. He looked at it now, still in tact, sitting on his shelf. He smiled and thought, "How lucky I am."

His anticipation of tomorrow began to grow as he continued to think of his past Christmas'. He gazed out into the accumulating snow, thinking about his family. He really never thought too much about them before. Most times he would just take it for granted like most kids his age. "But think about it," he thought. "I have a mom and dad, that's more than some kids, and two sisters. Sure they annoy me at times, but I do love them."

He continued to watch as the snow covered the trees and lawn. He saw a car make its way up the street through the new snow. It left a path behind it from its tires. He looked into the sky and saw the snow flakes falling. He was amazed at how soft and gentle it all seemed. He could hear music playing downstairs. His mom and dad were still awake and were listening to some Christmas songs.

As he continued to stare into the snow he could feel the breath of a small child standing next to him. He peered down to his left and saw his baby sister standing there holding her blanket and looking out his window, just like he was.

"Mikey, what that?" She said softly.

"That is snow," Michael responded.

"I like snow, it fun," she said back.

Michael agreed even though he knew she really didn't understand what it was. He remembered the first time she was in the snow and how much she had hated it.

"You should go to bed so Santa can come." Michael whispered into her ear.

She had a huge smile on her face and her eyes where as big as moons.

"Santa…, gifts?" "Wow! I sleep now, give me kiss."

Michael bent down and kissed her and she scampered off to bed in the room she shared with Michelle. Michael then went back and got in bed himself and closed his eyes thinking about what a lucky child he was to have such a good life. As the music began to fade in his mind, he fell asleep with the words from one of the songs his parents were listening to. "Christmas stays if we don't forget its meaning." Words that one day he would come to understand.

Chapter 7

THE HOLIDAY'S had ended and that always seemed to be depressing to Michael. He spent months looking forward to Christmas and New Year's and before he knew it, they had passed and the thrill was gone. When he returned to school after winter break, he couldn't believe how fast it had passed.

Michael did have a bit of hope for an exciting winter though, his dad had informed him that the base was just about ready and they would be leaving soon.

He had not told any of his friends at school of his plans. He felt it was better to wait until he was sure, before he told anyone. He was sure he wasn't going to miss all of the school work, and Molly, but he did feel bad about leaving Matthew and Tyler.

At the end of that week, Michael was on his way home from school when he noticed his mother and father in the garage. He thought that was very strange since they never got home before him. As he made his way into the garage, his dad turned and said, "How was school?"

Michael just responded with an, "Okay."

His mother had already gone into the house and Michael asked his dad, "What are you doing home already?"

"We are going to be leaving in a couple of days and I needed to do some things, so I left work early."

"Well, why is mom home?"

"She is not feeling well."

"Does that mean mom isn't going?"

"No, it just means she isn't feeling well, she's going!"

They walked into the house together and Michael kicked off his shoes and dropped his backpack. His dad was ahead of him and stopped in the kitchen to get a drink. Michael ran into the front room and then upstairs. He was looking for his mother to make sure she was okay to travel. It wasn't that he was concerned for her health, he was more concerned that the trip would be cancelled.

Michael found his mother in the bedroom and asked her if she was okay. She told him she was fine and that she only had a sore throat. He knew that with the weekend she would have time to get better.

She also asked Michael how school was today and he told her the same thing he told his dad. It was okay.

He turned to leave the room when he heard his dad call for him. He went down to the kitchen and his dad was sitting at the table looking at some pictures.

"Hey, do you want to see where we're going?" His dad asked.

"Yes!" Michael said as he jumped into a chair next to his dad.

"This is the building where the airplane will be parked, and this is the living areas, and this…"

"Wait a minute," Michael interrupted his dad's flipping of the pictures.

"What's wrong?" His dad said as he looked up at Michael.

"How did you get all of those buildings into the Arctic?" Michael had that confused look on his face as he looked back through the pictures.

"We brought them up there in sections, and assembled them on the site. The buildings were fabricated in Canada by a company that makes this type of structure. We just had to haul them up to the site and put them together."

"Like Lego's?" Michael questioned.

"Sort of, but much bigger, and the walls were already wired and piped for the utilities and water."

"Are we going to have bathrooms and things just like here at home?" Michael asked.

"Just like home," his dad said.

"What is the big antenna for in this picture?" Michael was pointing to one of the pictures laying on the table.

"That is what we will control the satellite with."

"Where do we get the electricity and power from?" Michael continued to ask questions.

"We have a couple of huge generators for the electricity, and we also have a really cool water system that uses the Arctic ice and snow for its supply. It is brand new and the only one in existence today." His dad was sounding like a kid with a new toy as he described the base to Michael.

His dad then handed him the stack of pictures and told him to look through them while he went to pick up his sisters at school. Michael took them and began to study them. He was amazed at how big some of the buildings were and how they had been built in the Arctic. He was becoming really excited about the trip and couldn't wait to leave.

He ran upstairs to show his mother the pictures, but she wasn't too excited and wanted to be left alone to rest her sore body. Michael just turned and left looking at the pictures the entire time.

It wasn't long before his dad was home with his sisters and he immediately began to show the pictures to Michelle and Kimberly. He was trying to explain them to the girls, like he was an expert on the buildings, but they didn't seem too interested in them.

He went back to where his dad was and wanted to know more about the buildings and when they were leaving. His dad went on to explain to him that they would be leaving sometime in the middle of next week. There were a few loose ends that needed to be tied up and then the other families needed to be notified about their departure date.

Michael was beginning to get excited about the whole thing and he couldn't help asking all kinds of questions about it. His dad seemed to be getting a little bit exasperated by all of the questioning. He had told Michael all about the way the buildings were put together and how the whole complex was sitting on an ice flow that was more than forty feet thick. He explained the way it moved with the ice and how the buildings contained a new material that made them more resistant to cold air. He told him about the water system and the heating system. When he was finished he looked at Michael and said, "You now know more about this place than any other human on the earth."

Michael wasn't sure what he meant by that, he was just

amazed at the whole thing and how he would soon be living in it.

The weekend went by quickly and before Michael knew it, Monday was here. He went to school and just couldn't concentrate on any of his work. All he could think about was the trip and going to the Arctic for a couple of weeks. He finally told his friends and they were all jealous, of course. It was not everyday that a young man got to go and explore the Arctic.

When he got home he hurried up to finish his homework and then went upstairs to start packing for the trip. He wanted to make sure he had everything he would need. He also was hoping he could sneak a few toys into his luggage.

When his mother got home, she told him she was feeling better and he was happy about that. It seemed like everything was coming together and now it was just a matter of waiting until the day they were to leave.

At dinner that night, his dad made a few comments about being ready to go and also told his family that they would be leaving the day after tomorrow. Michael couldn't believe it was really going to happen. He became really excited when his parents brought out the winter gear for the trip and started to pack all of their stuff. He had only to do one more day of school and then he was off on his adventure.

The next morning he was the first one up and was ready for school long before he needed to be. His parents were shocked that he was excited about going to school. What his parents didn't know, is that he was only excited because it was the last day of school, for a long while.

The day seemed to drag for Michael, but it finally ended and he made it home in no time. He was so excited he couldn't control himself and he kept acting silly. This seemed to bother his parents a bit, but they let it go, understanding that it was only his excitement.

At one point, his dad stopped him and said, "You may not be so excited when you get to this place, it is very cold and very dark. There is also not much to do."

Michael didn't care about all of that, what he cared about was no more school!

Finally, as he was sent to bed, his dad made one last comment to him, "I hope you are this happy when we get there, you may find it really boring."

But Michael knew somehow, there was going to be nothing boring about this trip.

Chapter 8

"HEY BUDDY, get up, it's time to go," a soft voice penetrated the morning air through the door of Michael's room.

Michael looked over at the digital clock on his night stand and the numbers read, 5:30. "Ohhh," he groaned.

"It's way too early, why are you waking me up?" Michael's voice was broken and harsh. He had a bit of a dry throat and he was really sleepy.

It was the day that they were scheduled to leave and the plane was due to depart the Air Base at 8:00 am. Michael's dad had gotten them up because it was going to be at least an hour drive to the base in traffic and there were many things to do before departure.

Michael stumbled out of bed and put on the pants and shirt that he had picked out last night. He was so excited yesterday and into the night that he had trouble sleeping. Now, when it was time, all he wanted to do was sleep.

He walked from his room and did his best not to fall down the stairs. He hit the floor at the bottom and could barely focus his eyes. He could see that it was still dark outside and it just seemed wrong to be up before the sun.

As Michael entered the kitchen, the lights were hurting his eyes, he squinted to see. His whole family was around the table having some donuts and juice for breakfast. His mother offered him some and he refused.

"This is the only thing we have and you may not eat for a while. So get it now." She explained to Michael, in the voice of a concerned mother.

"I need to wake up first, give me a minute" Michael mumbled to his mom.

Kimberly and Michelle were already eating and had a look of excitement on their faces. Michael's dad was busy getting his gear together and making sure the family had everything. He had explained to them earlier that there was a supply store where they could get some of the basics that they might run out of. They packed light, bringing only the things they would need for a couple of weeks. There was a laundry facility available at the base where they could wash their clothes if they needed to.

They also knew it was very cold there and while they were inside they would be wearing sweater shirts and long pants. If they did go out, they would put their snowsuits on over the top of their clothes.

They were all ready to go by 6:45 am so they headed out to the front yard where an Air Force van was just pulling up into their driveway.

"Good morning Colonel," the young man in the air force uniform addressed Michael's dad.

Michael's dad held the rank of a Colonel in the reserves. This meant he usually wore a silver eagle on his uniform.

But today, he was wearing a flight suit that had a name badge on the front with his name and rank on it.

Being the middle of January, it was very cold. The temperature was about twenty degrees Fahrenheit and there was snow covering the ground.

The kids were dressed in their warm winter clothes for the trip. Michael was wearing a coat, gloves, hat, and scarf. Michelle and Kimberly looked the same, they were all bundled up like they were going sledding.

They all piled into the van and Michael laid his head over to see if he could sleep some more. Kimberly loved to drive places and she sat up straight in her car seat and looked out the window at the view. The van then made its way to the highway and then north toward the base. Michael had no problem falling asleep, and he slept the whole way there.

Before he knew it, Michelle was waking him up. They were there! The hangar was open and inside sat a very large, gray, C-130 Hercules. Michael's dad had shown him pictures of this plane before, it was just like the one his dad was now flying for the Air Force, except this one looked different somehow. As they approached the hangar he could see what the difference was. It had big snow skis on the bottom where the wheels were.

"Dad, what are those for?" Michael asked as he pointed to them.

"That's so we can land on the snow." His dad said as he looked back to Michael.

The van pulled up into the opening of the hangar and they all got out. Gathered inside the hangar, were the other families that were going with them. Each of the families had some children. One family had a son who looked to be about Michael's age and he like to see that.

He thought how nice it would be to have someone to play with.

Another family had two little girls about Michelle's age and the third family had a boy and a girl that were younger than Michelle.

Michael's dad entered the hangar and looked around. He then turned to another pilot that was standing there and said, "Looks like we are ready to go, huh?"

The other officer nodded his head yes, and then motioned to a few people standing by the aircraft to go ahead and board.

Michael helped his mother and father get their bags from the van and as he walked around the plane he could see other bags laying on the ground under the wing.

"Just put them there," one of the airmen said as he pointed to the pile. Michael put down the bags and followed his dad around the plane.

"What are you doing?" He quizzed his dad.

"This is called a pre-flight walk around. I'm checking the plane for any obvious signs of something wrong. I also check the tires and flaps to make sure everything looks good."

"Can I help?" Michael asked.

"Sure, go ahead and look under the gear door to see if anything is leaking," his dad responded as he pointed to where the tires were.

Michael looked a bit confused as he turned back to look at his dad. He had no idea what a "gear door" was or where to look for one. Therefore, he just walked over to the plane and pretended to be looking at it.

"Everything okay?" His dad asked as he walked around the front of the plane.

"Yes, it looks great let's go!" Michael said as he followed his dad, running to catch up.

"Go ahead and help your mom get your sisters into the plane," his dad said as he continued around the plane looking at it very carefully.

Michael turned and walked over to his mother who was carrying Kimberly and said, "Let me have her, I'll put her in."

His mother gave her to him and then took Michelle by the hand as they walked up the couple of steps through the door and into the plane.

It was a large plane and it was very dull looking. Being a cargo plane there were not many esthetic qualities to it. Almost everything inside was grey or black or an ugly green and the seats were on a cargo pallet that was locked into the front cargo section.

Some of the families were already seated and buckling in. Michael put Kimberly into a seat on the end near one of the few windows on the plane. He then turned and looked around to see what else was on the plane.

The rest of the plane was full of pallets of supplies and equipment. There were a couple of fire extinguishers and some straps hanging on the walls. The floor was metal and had a lot of tie down rings attached to it. The only windows were in the doors and in the front where the pilots were sitting.

The ceiling contained a maze of wires and tubes with very few lights, which really didn't seem to make it too bright in the plane. It was kind of cold inside and there was a loud noise coming from the back. It sounded like an engine running or something. Michael had no idea what it was and when he asked his mom all she said was, "Huh?"

Exactly, he thought, we won't be doing much talking here if the plane is this loud even before the engines were running.

He continued to look around and saw some boxes that contained frozen foods. He was guessing it wouldn't be hard to keep the stuff frozen where they were going. There were also boxes of drink mixes, powdered milk, powdered eggs, vegetables, and all kinds of dried foods. He thought there was enough food to feed an army for a long time.

As he looked back to the rear of the plane, he saw one of the crew members placing their luggage on a pallet and tying it all down. He noticed that one of the bags had a tag that said Caution fire arms.

He didn't think too much about it at the time and continued to examine the aircraft. He found a ladder that went up to the top of the plane where there was a little door with a bubble window in it. He wanted to climb up and look out, but as he started too the door closed, and he heard his dad say, "Sit down!"

He turned and looked at his dad and pointing up asked, "Where does that go?"

"Up," responded his dad.

He started to laugh at the comment and then realized his finger was not pointing at the ladder, but straight up into the air at nothing. Embarrassed, he walked over and sat down in the seat between his mother and Kimberly. His mom was spreading a blanket and doing her best to introduce the family to the others over the noise in the plane.

All of the sudden the noise stopped and the lights went out. Michael's dad was standing on the steps to the cockpit, he held his hand up and said, "May I have your attention!"

After a brief pause he continued.

"We disconnected the power supply and they are going to be pushing us out of the hangar in just a minute. As soon as we are clear of the hangar I will start the engines and turn on the heat. It will take a few minutes to warm up and then you will be more comfortable."

Michael figured then that the noise he had heard was the portable power generator that was plugged into the plane. He recalled tripping over the cable as he was walking around with his dad.

Michael's mother took advantage of the silence to finish the introductions. She told each family her name and all of the children's names. She continued to explain that she was going to be their teacher and that brought lots of funny looks from all of the children. Evidently Michael wasn't the only one who thought he was out of school for awhile.

The plane began to move backwards and it became a bit lighter inside as the sun was shining in the few small windows. Michael looked over to show Kimberly the window and noticed she was asleep. Lucky girl, I hope I can sleep, he thought.

Soon, all four engines where running, and it became very loud inside the airplane. A young airmen who had introduced himself as the crew chief gave everyone some foam earplugs and showed them how to use them. They helped muffle the sound a little, but it was still impossible to talk to anyone.

Michael thought to himself that this must be an adults dream, the children couldn't talk them to death.

He felt the plane jerk forward and soon they were taxiing to the end of the runway. After a few moments, he could see out the window that they had turned parallel to the hangars and he guessed they must be on the runway.

He then heard the roar of the engines as they accelerated to full power and the plane lurched forward and began its run down the runway. He loved the feel of speed, just like the roller coasters at Disneyland. In just a few seconds, he could feel the gravity force push him into the seat, as the plane lifted off of the ground and headed into the sky.

The sound of the landing gear coming up made a loud noise and then they heard the sound of the hydraulic pumps that work the flaps, begin to groan. He could see the ground disappear below the plane as the clouds filled the window. He stretched to see out of the window, but it was too small and not easy to see out of.

"Well, we're on our way!" He screamed over the noise in the plane. His mother just smiled at him, not knowing what he had said.

The plane climbed and climbed and soon it started to get warm where they sat. Michael could see some of the people were asleep and others were reading or just sitting, staring off, daydreaming. He noticed his mother had a bag of chips or something that she was eating. She saw him look at her and she offered him some. He wasn't very hungry, so he just said no.

He was excited to be going on this trip and he couldn't sit still. He stood up and went over to where the steps led into the cockpit. The young man who was the crew chief stood near the steps reading a book. Michael noticed his name on his uniform, it said Sgt. Tim Campbell and in between the two words was 'Soup'.

Michael started to laugh and said to him, "Are you Campbell Soup?"

Tim smiled back at Michael and said, "That's my nickname."

"Oh I get it," Michael continued to laugh.

"Do you want to go up and see your dad?" Tim said to Michael.

"Can I?" Michael responded.

"Sure, just be careful not to touch anything."

Michael proceeded up the steps and onto the flight deck. He could see his dad sitting in the seat on the left, and another man whom he had seen outside the plane when they arrived was sitting on the right. A third man sat sideways on the back right looking at a really big board with lots of dials and gauges.

He took off his headset and said to Michael. "Come on in and have a look."

Michael was amazed at all of the instruments in the cockpit. Everything seemed so busy in there. The noise from the engines wasn't as bad up here and he could hear his dad talking into his mike that was on his headset.

"Climb and maintain flight level two three zero, Air Force 751." His dad must have been responding to the air traffic controller, he thought.

"What is flight level two three zero?" He asked out loud.

His dad heard him and turned around, motioned for Michael to come forward and as he lifted the headset off his ears he said, "Hey buddy what's up?"

Michael repeated, "What is flight level two three zero?"

His dad responded pointing to an instrument that

showed altitude, "That's twenty three thousand feet above sea level, that is how high we are."

Michael shook his head yes, as if he really understood, and then continued, "I wanted to get up and walk around and Tim said I could come up here."

"Sure you can, how is everyone doing back there?" His dad asked.

"Fine," Michael responded.

"Michael this is Major John 'Jack' Daniels," his dad pointing to the man sitting in the co-pilot seat.

Michael thought these nicknames were so silly and some of them were funny.

"How you doin' Michael?" Major Daniels greeted him.

"And that is Sergeant Banks," pointing to the man at the big console.

"What's up?" Sergeant Banks added.

"Nothing," Michael returned in his usual bored voice.

"Want to fly?" his dad said jokingly.

Michael grinned and then sat down in the other seat that was in the cockpit.

"We usually save that seat for special guests," Sgt. Banks joked.

"But, it is okay for you to sit there," his dad added.

"Are we there yet?" Michael asked.

"Nope… We are only over Philadelphia, and our next point to cross will be New York City. Then it is over Boston and onto our first stop in Goose Bay Labrador."

Michael laughed at the name, Goose Bay. Then Major Daniels showed him a map and sure enough right there in big red letters with an airport symbol was Goose Bay.

"After a short stop to refuel and eat we will continue to Greenland and then onto our final destination in the

Arctic." His dad was pointing to the map of the route they would be flying.

"Wow, how long is this going to take?" Michael asked.

"Well, it is about four more hours to Goose Bay and then another four to Greenland. After that it is only about two hours to the final destination."

"That is ten hours!" Michael said, using his math skills. "I won't say anything to the others," Michael whispered as if he had a secret to keep.

The three men smiled at Michael and his dad told him that the adults already knew how long the flight was going to take.

"As for you children, just relax and enjoy yourself," his dad said.

Chapter 9

THE STOP in Goose Bay seemed to fly by. They were there for three hours, but it seemed shorter. The plane was refueled and the kids got a chance to play in the snow. There was at least a foot on the ground when they arrived.

The adults had gone into a building after the plane was parked, and the kids stayed outside and played. Michael led the children in a snowball fight, and they built a snowman and a fort, all in the short time they were there.

They were a little upset when they were called in to eat. It was fun and their snowsuits worked great at keeping them warm.

Michael's dad explained during dinner, that it was only in the twenty's there and where they were going it would be much colder.

They all sat around a big table and ate a dinner that was prepared by the cooks on the Air Base.

After dinner, they checked out the weather report and went back on board the plane.

The plane left Goose Bay right on time. They were on

schedule and would be in Tulle, Greenland in about four hours.

The plane ride was becoming a little grueling, especially on the children. The noise and uncomfortable conditions made it difficult to sleep, read or do just about anything, but sit.

Fortunately for everyone it was going by fast. Michael spent most of his time on the flight deck with his dad and the other pilots. He enjoyed talking to them and watching what they were doing.

They were in and out of Greenland with no problem and soon all they could see out of the windows of the plane was ice, snow, and darkness of night. His dad had told him that the last leg of the flight would be about two hours depending on the wind and weather. Their final destination was inside the Arctic Circle near the North Pole. This was very exciting to Michael and he could not wait to get there. He continued to ask questions as they flew on and to his surprise, all of them were being answered. After about an hour, Michael decided to head back to where the others were in the plane to see if he could get some rest. He was enjoying the flight, but also was very tired from getting up so early that morning.

It seemed like just a few moments after Michael sat down and closed his eyes that he was awakened by his mother who was telling him to listen to his dad.

As they approached the base, Michael's dad had come to the seating area to give a last minute landing briefing to the passengers. Being that they were landing on snow and ice it was going to be different from a concrete runway. They needed to be aware of possible dangers. The plane was equipped with snow skis and that would allow it to land on the ice and snow. His dad had to let them know about how to exit the plane in case of an emergency. Michael was sure his dad was going to land the plane just fine, so he really didn't listen too well to the instructions.

He glanced at his mother and noticed there was a concerned look on her face. He asked her what was wrong and she just said she hated landings and wasn't too thrilled about landing on ice.

As they approached the landing site it was really dark and hard to see. Michael could hear the engines changing pitch and the plane was moving sideways as well as up and down.

"There must be a lot of wind," his mother said softly to herself grasping the armrest on the seat.

Michael reached over and took her hand to comfort her. She looked at him and smiled. She just couldn't believe how grown up he was becoming.

Up front, Michael's dad and co-pilot Major Daniels struggled with the controls to land as smooth as they could. Michael's dad had done this before and seemed to be confident in his ability to do it again.

The plane touched down with a soft thud. The skis were sliding in the snow and ice and the passengers could hear the engines reversing, which would slow the plane down. As the plane slowed, there was snow blowing all around in the darkness, only lit by the landing lights. Michael strained to look out the window, but there was nothing to see.

In the cockpit of the plane, the pilots had turned the plane around and were headed toward the large building that had been built as a hangar. The lights from the plane illuminated the huge doors and Major Daniels took a control from his bag and pushed a button. The doors began to open and they taxied into the entrance.

Ever so easily Michael's dad maneuvered the plane into the hangar and started to shut down the engines. The co-pilot, Major Daniels, came from the cockpit and told the passengers to sit tight while they got everything up and running in the building.

He exited the plane and walked over to a panel on the wall. He started to flip on the circuits and inside the hangar the lights began to come on. He then went over and pushed a button on the wall and closed the hangar doors. Michael's dad came from the flight deck and announced it was okay to exit the plane and join up in the hangar for a briefing.

One by one they exited the plane and onto the hangar floor under the wing. It was really cold in the building and some of the kids were shivering and holding their mothers. Michael's mother had Kimberly all wrapped up in a blanket and was clutching her close.

Michael came from the plane and looked around at the huge building they were standing in. It looked much like the airplane hangar at the base in Washington. It was big enough for the entire plane to fit in and there was room for other things. There was a huge tank that said Flammable on it sitting next to a bunch of tool boxes. There were pipes and wires in the ceiling and Michael was beginning to look around some more when he heard his dad begin to speak.

"Okay," Michael's dad began.

"Let's get this started. First of all the heaters have just been turned on and it is going to take some time to warm up. The temperature outside is minus thirty nine degrees

Fahrenheit. So as you can imagine it will take a while to get comfortable in here."

Everyone was looking around at the buildings in sort of amazement. It was hard to believe that this type of place could exist in the middle of the Arctic Ocean.

"We are going to lead you into the complex and turn on the systems as we go. Everyone should pay attention, so you know where all the switches and doors are. Also, make sure that you do not go outside by yourself." Michael's dad looked directly at him while making that comment.

They all followed Michael's dad into the first hallway off the side of the hangar. He explained each door and switch as they went in. He was also turning on lights and heat as the continued into the main buildings.

Each family was assigned their own living quarters, which on the inside looked much like a really expensive hotel. Each room had beds and sinks and there was even a little kitchen. They each had a TV and DVD players. Col. Rossi explained they did have satellite TV, but it wasn't very reliable.

"So far this is going to be great," Michael was thinking in his mind. "With a TV, DVD's, the snow, and no school... Who could ask for anything more?" he said out loud.

Everyone turned and looked at him and he got kind of embarrassed. His dad just turned and continued the tour.

They entered a really big room his dad called a day room. This room was where the kids could play, and would be attending school. There were TV's and radios and some books on the shelves. Right next to this room was a large dining area. His dad explained how they would meet for dinner here and have discussions on the progress being made.

"When do we get to go outside?" Michael asked.

"One step at a time Bud," his dad shot back.

As they walked around and looked at the buildings and rooms, Michael and his dad saw a beam of light piercing into a dark room.

"That's odd," his dad said.

"There isn't suppose to be any holes in these rooms and there is no light outside."

"Yes there is dad, there is a light on a pole," Michael responded to his dad's confused look and comment. He pointed outside through a window in the hall, at the light.

"Well, then how is it coming into this room?" His dad said as he continued to look puzzled.

"There is a hole in the wall near the top," Michael said as he pointed to where the light was shining through a very small hole.

"How did that get there?" His dad was beginning to sound a little annoyed that there was a hole in the wall. Not that a small hole is such a big deal, but with the freezing temperatures they didn't want any way for cold air to get in.

Michael walked over to the wall where the beam of light was touching it and he said to his dad, "Hey look, there is a hole over here too."

His dad walked over to where Michael was and sure enough there was a hole in the wall opposite the one in the outside wall.

"What could have done this?" His dad said as he rubbed his head.

"Aliens," Michael responded.

"Get out of here!" His dad said as he pushed him back into the hall.

"Go get Major Daniels," his dad ordered, and Michael turned and went to look for him.

A few moments later Michael returned with Major Daniels and announced to his dad, "Here he is!"

"Come and look at this," his dad said as he directed Major Daniels over to the outside wall with the hole in it. He then showed him the inside wall opposite with a hole and they both looked a bit confused.

"What could have done this?" Major Daniels asked.

"Aliens…!" Michael again was escorted from the room by his dad.

His dad re-entered the room and looked at the Major. His voice was serious and he was talking low, so no one could here him but Major Daniels.

"I think we have a problem," he started.

"That looks like a gun shot, like a bullet hole," he continued.

"A bullet hole? Who has a gun up here and who would shoot through the outside of this building." Major Daniels said with a very baffled look on his face.

"There is one way to find out, we need to locate the bullet in that wall." His dad said pointing at the inside wall of the room.

Michael stood in the hall and was watching and listening to all of this. He saw the concern on the faces of his dad and the Major. "What could be so wrong?" He thought to himself. "It just a little hole. Probably made by aliens, or maybe Inuit Indians. That is the only explanation for it unless Santa did it. Who else could be here?"

The two men then shut the door to the room and Michael couldn't see or hear what was going on anymore. His dad opened it once and asked Michael to go get the flight engineer Sergeant Banks. He did as he was told and soon all three men were in the room with the door shut.

Michael continued to stand in the hall like he was awaiting further orders, when his mother came by and asked where his dad was.

Michael pointed to the door and said, "In there. I think there looking for aliens."

She stopped and looked at Michael, "Are you nuts?"

"Why does everyone think I'm crazy?" Michael responded to his mother's statement. "There is a hole in the wall and no one lives up here, what else could it be?"

"Go and get ready for bed and check on your sisters!" His mother ordered.

She then went to the door and knocked on it. She could barely hear a voice ask who was there.

She said, "It's me, what are you doing?"

The door opened and she saw the three men looking at the wall.

"Is there something wrong?" she asked.

"Not sure," Michael's dad responded.

"There is a hole in the wall, and as you can see it is letting in light and air." Michael's dad pointed to the hole as he explained to his wife.

"We are going to have to go outside and fix this tomorrow. Then we must look for what or who could have done this." Major Daniels said as the others shook their heads in agreement.

"Tomorrow…, we will deal with this tomorrow. For now let's get some sleep," Michael's dad responded

It had been a very long day. It was nearly one in the

morning before they all turned and headed off toward their rooms. Michael's dad grabbed his mother's hand, and they walked to their room together.

When they entered the rooms the kids were laying on the bed watching a movie on DVD.

"This is a cool room," Michelle said as she saw her parents enter.

"I like the bed and the DVD's, can we stay longer?" She continued.

"Let's just get through a couple of days first before we start making plans to stay longer," their mother said to the kids.

"Get ready for bed and let's get some sleep," added their dad.

The three kids went into the bathroom and they all brushed their teeth and put on the winter pajamas that they had brought. They came out and got into bed. Michelle and Kimberly shared a room and Michael had his own room. Their mom was there to kiss them all goodnight and she tucked them in.

Michael was surprised at how cold it was in the buildings. His dad had explained how the heating system worked, and how they would be colder at night. But this, this was cold. He climbed under the covers and felt like an animal burrowing into a hole. He pulled the covers up and even covered his head. As he lay there, he could feel the warmth of the down comforter and the flannel sheets. He was happy they were working as advertised. He also could hear his mother talking to his sisters.

"Mom, how do we know when it is morning, if it's always dark here?" Michelle asked as she pulled up the covers.

"I will come and get you in the morning, don't worry," her mother responded. She didn't tell her it was already morning.

As she exited their room, she turned off the light and the kids closed their eyes and fell right to sleep, exhausted from the long day of flying.

It wasn't too long after that, that Michael's mom and dad were sound asleep, also exhausted from the long day.

Chapter 10

THE NEXT morning, around eleven, the residents of the Arctic lab began to wake up. It was hard to tell the time since it was dark most of the time, but the clocks in the rooms told everyone a new day had dawned.

Michael and his family woke up and gathered in the kitchen area to have some breakfast. That became the first interesting part of living in this new place. All of the food was dried, powdered, or frozen. The choice for breakfast was either dry cereal and powdered milk, or hot cereal. Michael and Kimberly liked to have oatmeal back home, so they chose the hot cereal made in the microwave. Michelle opted for the dried cereal and milk. One of the best parts of the breakfast was that their mother had made them all some hot chocolate. It tasted good and felt good on this very cold morning.

After breakfast they met the other families in the large day room for a morning briefing. They had been told that each day at eight in the morning they would have a daily meeting to go over the day's schedule. But today it was moved up to noon, since they had such a short night. Because of not getting to bed until after one in the morning, it was not logical to expect everyone to get up at seven for a meeting.

Everyone had assembled and they all had a look of excitement for what they were doing. All of the kids were smiling and talking to each other. The adults had coffee and were sitting in groups having their own conversations. Next to the large coffee pot someone had hung a sign that said, "Starbucks".

Michael's dad stood up in the front of the room and began the meeting. He started by telling everyone about some of the day's activities. They included the first school day for the children and some of the computer work that needed to be done. He didn't say anything about the hole and Michael once started to ask, but his dad stopped him and told him to just wait until later.

After the meeting, the children stayed in the room and Michael's mother began to explain how school would be run, but Michael wasn't listening, he was watching his dad and the other men talk about the hole.

"I want to go with them," he thought to himself.

And just then, as if he was still back in his middle school, he heard those words.

"Michael, are you paying attention?"

"Yes," he said as he quickly turned his head to look at his mother.

She stood there glaring at him for a moment and then went back to the directions. Michael could not concentrate on her because he was absorbed by the problem that his dad was dealing with.

"Man, I want to go with them," Michael thought again, as he saw the men leave the room and head down the hall.

If anyone was capable of solving this problem it was Michael. He was an explorer and a scientist. He knew his way around the outdoors, he could problem solve, and he had good eyes for finding things others couldn't.

Instead, here he was sitting in a boring classroom listening to lectures and taking notes. He paused for a moment and hoped his mother couldn't read his mind as he was thinking these thoughts.

"This is not the stuff for heroes like me," he whispered to himself.

After what seemed to be forever, the class was over and Michael was given the freedom to roam around and check the place out. He went down a hall and into the airplane hangar and there next to one of the walls were several snowmobiles.

"Oh yeah! I want to ride these," Michael said out loud.

"Not yet your not!" came his dad's voice from next to the plane.

"Come on dad let's take them out!" he replied.

But his dad went on to point out to him that they were not there for winter sports, but to do a job, and the snowmobiles were for emergencies only. "We only want to go out with them if we need to. Besides it is really cold out there and you could freeze." Michael knew that his dad was just saying that so he would stop asking to use them.

"Well, can we just see if they work?" Michael continued to nag at his dad.

"Not now and maybe not ever. They are here for emergencies and not to play on," his dad said, reiterating what he had said earlier.

"Dad, did you find out what caused the hole in the wall?"

"Not yet, but we're not through looking yet. We went out for a few minutes earlier, but we didn't see anything unusual."

"Can I go out with you next time?"

"Well, I don't know… if it's okay with your mom then…"

"Alright I get to go!" Michael said as he turned and ran back toward the door.

"Hey wait! I didn't say it was okay!"

But it was too late, Michael had disappeared down the hall and into the main building.

"Well, I guess I'll just have to explain this to his mother later," Michael's dad said to no one, as he was alone in the hangar.

He left the hangar and made his way to the room with the rest of the family. Michael's mother was there and asked how his day was. Before he could answer Michael interrupted with the news that he was going outside with his dad. His mother just looked at him with a blank look and then looked at his dad.

"Are you crazy? It is way to cold for him outside and I don't think that is a good idea!"

"We can go for a few minutes, it will be okay."

"And what do you do when he gets frostbite?"

"What is that?" Michael interrupted.

"He won't," his dad replied to his mother.

"What is this frostbite?" Michael asked again.

"It is what you get for being crazy and going outside when it is cold." His mother said sarcastically.

"Frostbite isn't caused by being crazy, only irresponsible," his dad added.

"I will protect him and so will all of the winter gear we have for working outside. He will be just fine," his dad said as he continued to plead his case. It was clear Michael got all of his negotiation skills from his dad.

"Well, I don't think it is a good idea and I hope you know what you are doing." His mother seemed to be a bit upset, but it looked as though Michael was going to be able to go outside with his dad after all.

As he began to realize this, his sister Michelle came into the conversation and asked, "Can I go too?"

Michael was quick to point out that it was no place for a little girl and she would get frostbite. As if all of the sudden he was an expert on this subject.

His mother interrupted the conversation and said that it was almost time to go and meet the others for dinner and the kids needed to go and get ready.

As she turned to leave to get ready herself, her last words to them were, "And no fighting!"

Chapter 11

THE FIRST full day in the complex was nearing an end and the families met for dinner in the big room. The kitchen in this room was big enough to prepare a large meal and the plan was for everyone to meet for dinner there and discuss the day's events. All of the adults worked together to prepare the meal and the kids were going to take turns setting the table and cleaning up. It just so happened that the first night it was Michael's turn since he was the oldest.

The table was large and Michael asked his sister to help. She wasn't really thrilled about it, but her mom told her too. She reluctantly began to help and basically all she did was rearrange what Michael had already done.

This was beginning to get on Michael's nerves, and his mother had noticed this too so she walked over and told him to just ignore what Michelle was doing.

That was about right Michael thought, it seemed like everyone except him got a free pass when it came to doing the wrong thing. This confirmed to him that life wasn't fair.

They sat down and ate dinner and there were so many conversations it was actually hard to keep up. All of the children were talking at the same time trying to tell their parents about their day and the adults were in the process of having a serious conversation about their day too.

It was impossible to get in a word, so Michael just sat there and ate. They were having spaghetti which was one of his favorites, therefore, he just used his mouth for eating and let them do the talking. When he finished his first bowl of spaghetti he asked for another. His mom told him to help himself. He smiled and went to the stove and filled his plate again. It seemed like he was the only one enjoying this dinner.

When dinner was over, everyone pitched in and helped clean up. Michael was wondering where all this help had been before dinner.

Soon the room was clean and everyone had moved on to their living quarters. That left Michael and his dad sitting alone in the large room.

"Dad, am I going outside with you tomorrow?" Michael said. He was eager to get into the snow and ice.

"I don't know, we have to see if we can get your mother to okay it," Michael knew his dad was just stalling, his mom had nothing to do with okaying anything here.

"But dad you said I could go out and help you," Michael began to nag. "I heard you tell mom I would be okay in my winter gear."

"When did I say that?" His dad asked.

"Today, when you were in the airplane hangar, and then again in our room."

"I did?"

"Yes you did!"

"Well then I guess I had better keep my word and let you go outside tomorrow."

Michael couldn't believe what he just heard his dad say. He was actually winning this argument?

What he didn't know was that his dad had been planning on taking him outside to help with fixing the hole in the building anyway.

"But first…"

"Oh no here we go," Michael thought.

"You have to do something for me." His dad continued.

"Here it comes…"

"First you have to go to bed and get a good nights sleep and then be ready in the morning."

"That's it, just go to bed and be ready. Wow! I can do that, goodnight!" Michael tore off down the hall toward his room.

In the morning Michael was the first one to wake up. He jumped out of bed and ran into his parent's room calling for his dad. He was very excited to finally be doing what he had dreamed of doing, going into the Arctic and exploring it.

"I'm ready, can we go?" Michael's excitement was overwhelming at seven o'clock in the morning.

"Easy Buddy, we have all day," his dad's voice was still heavy with sleep.

His dad looked up and noticed Michael was already dressed in everything but his snow suit and boots.

"You got dressed fast," his dad commented.

"I slept in this last night," Michael said as he looked down at his clothes.

"Please tell me your lying," his mother's voice came out from under the covers.

"But I didn't want to be late and I wanted to…"

Michael's voice was drowned out by his mother talking to his dad, or should I say, questioning his dad about the day.

"You're not really letting him outside, are you?"

"I promised him, and I can use the help fixing the hole in the wall."

"If anything happens to him…!" His mom's voice became rather serious.

"Nothing will happen, he will be all covered up and we won't stay outside long." His dad's voice seemed to be reassuring, but his mother wasn't buying it.

At that point Michael realized he had better get out of the room before minds were changed and he missed his outdoor adventure. He turned and went back down the hall to his room. On the way, he stopped by the kitchen and got a breakfast bar from the cupboard.

After a few moments he heard his dad in the kitchen, he went there to talk to him to make sure he was still going with him.

As he entered, his dad looked at him and winked. He said, "Don't worry I took care of it, you're going with me."

Michael got a big smile on his face and he could feel the excitement growing inside of him.

"Alright, when do we go?"

"In a little while, I have to do some things first. I will come and get you when it's time, until then you can help your mother."

"What, I thought…"

"Go!" his dad's voice echoed across the kitchen.

Michael turned and went into the room with his mother to see what he could do to help her, talking to himself the whole way. She was cleaning up and looking for clothes to dress Kimberly in.

"Dad said I need to help you," Michael said to his mother.

"Go and help your sister clean up the bedrooms." His mother said.

Michael was very confused. He thought he would be going outside this morning and instead he was cleaning. "Man its rough being a child in today's world," he thought.

After a short time, Michael's dad returned and told him they were ready to go. Michael became so excited he started running around and yelling like some kind of maniac.

"Get your stuff together and head for the hangar," his dad told him.

It only took Michael a few moments to get all dressed up and he bolted for the hangar. When he got there his dad and the other pilots were already there going through some equipment. Major Daniels went into the plane and came back out with the bag that was marked firearms. Michael knew what was in it and he asked his dad if they were going to be shooting something.

His dad explained to him that the guns were just a precaution in case they needed to protect themselves.

"From what?" Michael said with a loud confused voice.

"You never know what we might run into out there," his dad answered.

Then Michael's dad began to check out his clothes to make sure he was all buttoned up and safe to go outside. They were all wearing their cold weather suits. Their underclothes had warmers in them that were operated by a small battery pack. Over that, they wore a snowsuit that was all white and very warm. They put their hats on their heads that pulled down over their faces and then over that, a fur covered hood.

Michael made sure his hat was on correctly and his dad then gave him an ear piece and a microphone that he attached to his belt.

"This is so we can communicate while were outside," his dad instructed him.

When he turned it on Michael could here his breathing and then he could hear the voices of everyone who was going with him. They started to run checks on the microphones and each one said check 1, check 2, and as it continued Michael started with his own check.

"Check one, two, three, four, is anybody listening?" Michael was obviously joking around.

His dad told him to just listen, and if he needed help to speak clearly and they would hear him. His dad put on his gloves and told Michael to do the same. They were mittens, and they fit over a regular pair of gloves with fingers. After that, they did a final check to see if everyone was ready.

Michael told him he was getting warm in all of the clothes and his dad just said, "Be patient, it will be cold soon."

The last thing he did was give Michael a pair of goggles for his eyes. They had this liquid stuff in them that his dad said would keep him warm.

"It is liquid warmth, it will keep your eyes warm so you can see while we're outside."

Michael put them on and almost instantly he could feel warmth on his face.

"These are great!" Michael said.

He heard his dad on the radio as he said, "It's time to go, follow me." Michael followed him to the door of the hangar and he paused for a moment until the others caught up.

His dad opened the door to the outside and stepped through it. Michael followed close behind and soon found himself in the dark, cold wasteland of the Arctic Circle.

"Wow, this is weird," Michael said into his mike.

"Follow me and stay close," his dad replied.

Michael followed his dad around the hangar and to the side of the building where they lived. His feet were in heavy boots and the weight made the snow and ice crunch under them as he walked. He passed by a window where he could see inside and he saw his mother and sisters as well as some of the others looking out at them. He was doing his best to make faces at them, but he was hidden inside of all of the clothes and goggles on his face. As he walked, he paid no attention to where he was and he walked right smack into a metal pole.

"Arrgh" he said as he backed away from it.

"What did you do?" his dad asked.

"I bumped into this pole," Michael replied.

"Will you please watch where you're going!"

Michael looked over and could see everyone in the window laughing at him, so he just looked back and took a bow. He was always entertaining everyone and used his clumsiness to his advantage.

He looked back at the pole, thought for a moment, and then pulled the hat he had over his face up a bit to expose his mouth. He began to stick his tongue out as he leaned toward the pole.

His dad yelled, "No! Do not stick your tongue to that pole!"

He looked at his dad for a second and then put his tongue back in his mouth and pulled the hat back down. He wondered if his tongue would get stuck, but he would have to wait until later to test this hypothesis.

He went back to following his dad and as he did he looked back at the pole and saw that it was lit by a spot light. At the top was an American flag flapping in the breeze and the snow that was being blown around by the wind. He felt himself walk into something else and then realized it was his dad who had stopped.

"Will you watch where you are going please!" his dad said with a bit of annoyance.

"Sorry dad, I was just looking at the flag."

"Okay, but be careful what you are doing and where you are going. It is dangerous out here."

"Hey dad, why does that flagpole have holes in it?" Michael said into the radio and everyone at once looked at him and then the pole.

His dad walked closer to it and gazed up at the pole. He noticed something and motioned for Major Daniels and Sergeant Banks to look as well. Major Daniels had a weapon with him, it was an M-16, and he took it off his shoulder and held it across his body.

"What is going on?" Michael asked.

"Those are bullet holes Michael, just like the one in the wall," his dad returned into the radios. "I guess we have a bigger problem then I first thought," he continued.

Michael was unaware that yesterday his dad and the major had dislodged the bullet from the wall where he had seen the hole. It was a high powered rifle bullet and it was not from hunters. His dad had been able to determine it was from a foreign country because of the markings on it, and now there were more holes in the pole outside of the room.

Michael's dad then said, "I guess whoever did this was shooting at the building and missed a few times. See where the holes go across toward the building and then the one that hit the building is right in line."

The light that they saw in the room was from the flag pole and now Michael was beginning to understand all of the confusion and nervousness he had seen over the last two days.

"Dad, who could be shooting at us?" Michael asked.

"I hope no one is shooting at us, let's hope this is all a mistake," his dad replied.

"Let's just get this completed and head inside before we get too cold, we can figure this out later," his dad continued, looking a bit nervous.

They walked over to the wall and Michael's dad took a tube of something out of the bag he was carrying.

"Hold this ladder for me will ya Bud," his dad said as he put a small step ladder against the wall of the building.

Michael's dad climbed up a few steps on the ladder and opened the tube. He then squirted something into the hole that expanded and then immediately froze and hardened.

"What is that stuff?" Michael said.

"It's a sealer for this hole," his dad replied.

Michael then thought he heard the sound of an engine. It was a strange sound way out here in the darkness. All the sounds he could hear were the wind, and the radio, and now this engine sound seemed to be getting closer.

He looked off in the distance and thought he saw a faint light.

"That's strange," he said.

"What?" his dad replied.

Before he could say anything he saw the snow jump up from the ground and he heard the sound of metal hitting metal. It was a kind of pinging sound, like when he would pound on his bike with a hammer.

"Look dad the snow is jumping up," Michael said as he looked up.

But before his dad responded and before Michael could react, his dad jumped off of the ladder and on top of him. He could feel the weight of his dad on top of him and he did not know why.

He was helplessly frozen in the snow. His mind was racing, trying to figure out what was happening. Why had his dad jumped on top of him?

"What are you doing?" Michael struggled to talk under the pressure of being held down.

As he felt the weight leave him, he struggled to his feet and just stood there. As he began to look around he saw a light disappear in the distance. He then heard that engine sound again. He also heard something else, it was the sound of Major Daniels firing the weapon he had in the direction of the light. Michael could see the others in the window watching all of this and he knew that they had no idea what was going on. He had no idea what was going on either.

Michael looked at his dad and did not know what to do. He realized that he may have just been shot at by someone. The snow hadn't been jumping up, those were bullets hitting it, he thought, and hitting it just a few inches from where he stood. The metal sound was the bullets hitting the wall of the building, and he saw the building and the window and all of the sights filled his mind.

"Dad, what are we supposed to do now?" This question echoed across the empty frozen landscape like a public address announcer at a ball game. "I'm not sure," replied Michael's dad standing a few feet away and looking off into the distant darkness.

This wasn't exactly the answer Michael was expecting. He was looking for a reason why all of the sudden his whole life was in danger. In his mind, his thoughts were of what could be an exciting adventure. Instead, it was nothing like he had imagined. 'Nothing is certain in this world, or in one's life.' That is what his dad had always told him, and now he was seeing it in reality.

To go from the protected comfort of his home, to having this uncertainty in the middle of this frozen wasteland, in such a short time was a big shock to him. It was then he realized it must also be a shock to the other people, who were with him, and he looked at them…, as they looked back from the window, he saw their faces… He saw the concern and the fright on them. It was at that moment he realized it was up to him to save these people and maybe the rest of the world.

Chapter 12

"Who was shooting at us?" Sergeant Banks yelled into the radio.

"I don't know," was the puzzled reply from Major Daniels.

"Is everyone okay?" Michael's dad asked.

In turn each man replied, "Yes." Even Michael said yes, though he knew his dad wasn't talking to him. They were all a bit startled.

Michael's dad looked around and seemed to be very confused about what had just happened. He looked at Michael and leaned over to brush some of the snow off of his suit.

"Are you sure you're okay?" He asked.

"Yeah, but why did you jump on me?"

"Those were bullets hitting the building next to you, didn't you know that?"

"No…, well…, maybe. I thought it was just snow or ice or something…" Michael was stuttering through his thoughts, and his voice seemed nervous.

"Well, since we're finished with what we had come outside to do and seeing that there aren't any more holes in the building, let's head back in," Michael's dad was trying to minimize the fright he had of nearly having his son shot.

On the way back, all Michael could think about was why he wasn't having any fun on this trip. He was cold and a little bit nervous about what had happened. He really didn't know how close he had just come to being shot by whomever it was that was shooting at them.

They reached the door of the hangar and Michael entered first to a swarm of people waiting to find out what had just happened. His mother grabbed him and pulled off his hat and eye wear.

"Are you okay?" she asked frantically.

"I'm fine mom, let me go!" Michael responded as he pulled away from her to get out of his clothes.

His dad entered last and was met by a flurry of questions.

"What is going on?" Michael's mother asked.

"I'm not sure, but someone else is up here and for some reason they don't want us to be here with them," his dad was doing his best to explain the situation without making it sound serious.

"Well, what was that hitting the building and why did you jump on Michael and why was Major Daniels firing his weapon…?" The questions just kept coming.

"Alright one thing at a time!" his dad replied.

"First, let us get out of these clothes and get inside to warm up, then we can try to answer all of your questions," his dad continued.

The others in the group were just standing there listening like he was a tour guide explaining a museum to them. They were not sure what to do or say, so they all just stood and listened to the exchange between Michael's mom and dad.

"What is going on?" Michael's mother was at the end of her patience. "This was supposed to just be a few weeks in the Arctic to do some simple computer work and then back home to continue with our lives, and all of the sudden our lives are in jeopardy?"

"All I know is that we are not alone up here," Michael's dad started to try to make sense of the whole thing. "I don't know who those people are and I am not sure why they would just shoot at us randomly like that. But one thing is for sure, we need to figure this out and fast."

Michael could see the concern on his dad's face. He also could see that the others in the group were also looking a little scared and concerned. The other children were not there and Michael was the only child that knew what was going on.

"It was probably a good thing he thought," the other kids would be scared.

"What do we do first?" Major Daniels stepped forward to ask the question.

"First, we secure this area," Colonel Rossi said. "Next, we are going to have to figure out who these people are and why they are up here with us. According to our intelligence there is no one within five hundred miles of this location."

"What intelligence, is there something we are not being told?" Michael's mother looked at his father with the look of a person who felt like they were not given all of the information that they needed.

Michael and the others continued to stand and listen as if they were watching a tennis match. Except it was not a game. Everyone was concerned for the safety of the group. If someone was shooting at them, the danger was quite real and needed quick action.

"Okay everyone, let's head inside and see if we can figure this out where it is a bit warmer," Michael's dad was trying his best to calm their fears. It was kind of like the airline pilot who tells the passengers, in a very calm voice, that they are experiencing a slight problem, when an engine has fallen off.

The group headed inside and began to mill around in the great room. It was only three in the afternoon. Too early to eat and no one was very hungry anyway. Michael's dad came in with the other pilots and looked around at the group. Major Daniels was still carrying his weapon and now Sergeant Banks had also picked one up.

"Is it really necessary for these men to be carrying weapons inside?" Michael's mother took the initiative to ask.

"It is only a precaution. We are going to be setting up a watch and some extra security measures while we try to sort this out," Michael's dad answered. "The thing we must do first is to remain calm. We must stay together and no one is going outside until further notice."

"Great," Michael thought. "I get outside for ten minutes and it ruins the whole trip."

Michael stood next to his mother as he watched with great anticipation to see what his dad was going to do next. He began to review the situation and he realized that if he could think of a way to help, he would. His mind was all a blur, he was seeing all of the sights and sounds of what had happened outside.

He then had a thought and began to speak, "Hey dad, those guys were on snowmobiles, right?"

"What do you mean, Michael? How do you know that?"

His dad turned his attention to Michael as did everyone else. For the first time on this trip he had finally said something important.

"The sound and the light," Michael returned comment.

"What sound and what light?" His dad questioned as he moved closer to him.

"Right before the shots I saw a light and heard an engine sound."

"He is right," Major Daniels butted in as he stepped forward. "I heard it as well and I also saw the light. That is what I was shooting at."

"Well, then that means that they must be staying close. It would not be possible for them to travel a long distance up here on snowmobiles," his dad was now standing next to Michael, as he spoke. "Let's take a look at the map in the computer room," he continued. "And Michael you come with me."

Michael was very surprised that he was invited to the map reading with his dad. It's not like he was an adult or even someone who could help, but his dad was pleased with his observations and wanted him to continue to help out.

His dad, the major, and the other two flight crew members walked toward the computer room and Michael followed close behind.

As they left the room, Michael turned to the others and said, "Don't worry I have it under control."

His mother just shrugged and half chuckled. His sister Michelle, who had just came into the room, was really confused about what was going on and she turned to her mom and said, "What's for dinner?"

Her mother just turned and walked away.

In the computer room Michael's dad had laid out a map of the camp and the surrounding area. He pointed out that the map showed an area of fifty square miles. He figured that was good enough since most snowmobiles only have about that much fuel for a round trip. He also pointed out that in these temperatures, it would take too long to go any further and whoever was on the snowmobile would freeze to death.

"We start here," Michael's dad pointed to the location on the map where Michael had said he saw the light.

Major Daniels agreed, "That is where I saw it as well."

While the men bent down to get a closer look at the map detail, Michael noticed a computer in the room. It was on, and it was showing a satellite location over the Arctic. In the middle were a bunch of dots and the words "Base 1".

"Hey, what does this mean?" Michael asked as he pointed to the screen.

"That is just one of the satellites taking infrared photos of the base. See, that is us right there inside of the square," his dad said as he turned to answer Michael and he looked at the screen, pointing to the dots.

"Well, if this satellite can see us, could it see others?" Michael asked.

Michael's dad just stood there for a moment and then looked at Michael and said, "That is amazing!"

"What?" Michael said with a confused look.

"How do you know this stuff, Bud?" Michael's dad got a big smile on his face... "We can use the satellite to find them!" His dad said and he put his arm around Michael. "I guess they teach you more than I thought in that school," He rubbed Michael's head as he grinned.

"That is brilliant, we have the satellites and the ability to do this," Major Daniels became excited as he walked over to the computers and sat down at a keyboard.

"Right out of the blue, you thought of that, right out of the blue." Michael looked at his dad as he said this and wasn't sure what he meant.

"Dad, it is dark outside how did I think of this out of the blue?"

"It's a figure of speech Michael and it means out of nowhere."

"It wasn't out of nowhere it was out of my head."

"That's what I said, out of the blue," Michael's dad smiled and turned to the screen.

Major Daniels was typing in some coordinates to see if he could position the satellite to look around the area.

"With the infrared sensors on the satellite we should be able to pick up some sign of life, if there is any, in this frozen place," Major Daniels was talking as he typed.

After a few minutes they were all staring at the screen as the satellite image moved across the Arctic. All that was visible was white snow, and some ice flows.

"Stop, right there!" Michael's dad was pointing to some red dots on the screen as the satellite moved and Major Daniels pressed some keys and stopped the satellite.

The image froze on the screen and there it was. Only about ten miles from their camp was an image of a tent with a bright orange fire in it and three smaller infrared images of people. Outside was the image from the exhaust of the snowmobiles.

"No doubt about it, that's them!" Michael's dad said as he again pointed to the screen.

"But, who is them?" Major Daniels replied.

"That's what we are going to find out," Michael's dad said as he leaned over the screen. He then directed Major Daniels to mark the location and continue to monitor the site using the satellite.

He turned and looked at Michael and said again with a big smile, "Good work, Bud!"

Michael felt proud. For the first time in his life he had done something with real meaning. He had no idea how that thought about the satellite had come to him, but it did. He was very happy to see his dad smile at him and knew his mom would also be proud.

"Man, I finally get some respect," he said to himself as he turned to go out of the room.

"What do you want to do first?" Major Daniels addressed the Colonel.

"First we get organized. Next, we make a plan. And finally, we execute the plan and fix this problem," Colonel Rossi was showing the educator in himself as he spoke.

"We need to get one of the computer programmers in here to work with you," he told the major. "Then I will take the two sergeants with me and we will do a little recon of our own. You guys can watch the monitor and keep us informed of any movement and also of how close we are to them. I think we will try to get close enough for a good look without them seeing or hearing us. Maybe two miles from them on the snowmobiles and then we walk the rest of the way. It's wide open out there so we will need some stealth."

The others were listening intently to the Colonel's ideas.

When he stopped Major Daniels added, "Good thing it's dark most of the day. We can go at any time."

"Well that is it then, we go early in the morning tomorrow, maybe catch them while they sleep," and Michael's dad turned to leave the room. As he exited he left one last order, "Don't let them out of your sight!"

Chapter 13

THE REST of the day went by without incident and the group met for dinner in the large room. Everyone was waiting for some information on what was going on. Michael's dad didn't say much. The meal was eaten in mostly silence and then at the end, the children got up and left except for Michael, he stayed to listen as his dad stood up to speak.

"I just want everyone to relax. We have the situation under control at this time."

Not everyone was as confident as the Colonel, but they listened and gave him a chance to explain what had happened and what they were going to do next.

Michael sat and looked across the room at the window on the other side of the building. He could see some snow blowing around in the light outside the window and it made him think of that last Christmas Eve and how happy he was. He thought it would be nice to be there again and have that same feeling. Instead, he was filled with confusion and a little bit of fear. Whoever it was that was shooting at them meant business and he didn't want anything to happen to his family or any of the others with them. He turned toward his dad and listened as he spoke.

"We know that there is someone else in our general area. We know that for some reason, a reason that I cannot explain, they have been shooting at the building and today, us."

He continued to explain that they had located a camp nearby with the help of a satellite and they were planning on going out to see who it was. Michael's dad did his best to calm the nerves of the others and his own family, but there was still a feeling of uneasiness in the room.

Michael's mother was not very happy about the whole situation and she spoke, "I think we should just load up the plane and leave."

"We can't do that right now," his dad said back.

"Why?"

"Because it is our job to finish this site work and anyway we stand a risk of being shot at in the plane. We need to find out who it is and stop them."

"Then call for help."

"It wouldn't help if we did. The only way up here is by flying the plane we have in the hangar."

"What are you saying, the only plane able to make this flight is here, in the hangar? What kind of an operation is this?"

Michael could tell his mother was getting very upset and he knew that wasn't a good thing. He had seen his mother get upset with him and his sisters and he never liked it. But this was different, she was getting mad at his dad, for feeling like she and her family had been put at risk.

"Mom, we can stop these people and make this work,"

Michael spoke in a calm voice. The calmness of his tone even surprised his mom and she looked over at him.

"What do you mean, we? You're not going anywhere."

"But dad said I could help him find these people and…"

"I don't care what your dad said, you are not going anywhere!"

Michael looked at his dad, but his dad just turned and walked toward the door. Michael guessed he felt the conversation was going nowhere and decided to leave. Except he didn't leave he just shut the door.

Michael wanted to say something, but he didn't know what to say or how to say it, so it would not get him into any more trouble.

"Look, I know what we can do to solve this problem and you just have to trust me," his dad said quietly.

"I did trust you and look where we are now," his mother responded with a bit of sarcasm.

"We can't just sit here and do nothing," his dad continued.

"I'm going to bed," his mother said as she stood up to leave.

"And you're coming with me," she added as she pointed to Michael.

His dad just gave him a smile and said goodnight. Michael walked out of the room with his mother and went into their living quarters to get ready for bed. His two sisters were already in their pajamas and were sitting on the couch in the room watching a movie on DVD.

"What's going on?" Michelle asked Michael as he entered the room.

"Nothing, we have to go to bed now."

"But the movie isn't over!"

"Mom said for us to go to bed so you better turn it off."

"Mom!" Michelle yelled through the door to their parent's room.

"Do we have to go to bed now?" She added.

"In a minute," came the reply through the door.

"See, I told you," Michelle said as she turned to look at Michael and stuck her tongue out at him.

Michael did nothing in return. He was a little bit depressed over all of the events of the day. All he wanted to do was to go to sleep and hope that tomorrow would be better.

Meanwhile, back in the great room, Michael's dad and the other men from the group were continuing their meeting. They were trying to work out the details for an early morning raid on the camp of strangers. As they finalized their plans, the Colonel began to review what they were going to do.

"It is set then, we do this at zero-four-hundred. I will go with Sergeants Banks and Campbell. I am also going to be taking my son Michael. Major Daniels you will work the computer with the help of Mr. Franks."

Mr. Franks was one of the computer programmers who had come to help set up the computer system. His knowledge of computers would be a help to Major Daniels while he was using the satellite to track the movement of the strangers.

"Let's get some sleep and we meet at oh-four-hundred in the hangar." Michael's dad ended the meeting and the men all set out to their living quarters to try to get some sleep. Michael's dad entered the room and walked over to the bed where Michelle had fallen asleep watching the movie. He bent down and covered her up and kissed her goodnight. He then walked over to Kimberly who had been asleep for a while and kissed her goodnight. He then looked at Michael, who was lying on the couch staring at the ceiling.

"You better get some sleep Bud if you're going to be of any help to me tomorrow."

"What?" Michael seemed a bit confused.

"You're going with me tomorrow," his dad said.

"But mom said…"

"I know what your mom said, but I need you tomorrow, I need your help."

Michael could not believe his ears, had the cold temperatures froze his dad's brain? Had his dad just lost his mind in all of the excitement? Michael did not know how to react. If he did have the chance to go he was excited, but for some reason he couldn't believe what he had heard. He went off to bed not fully sure he would be going anywhere tomorrow. He also wasn't sure if he wanted to go with his dad. It could be dangerous out there.

Four in the morning came rather quickly in the cold, dark, Arctic and Michael was not quite sure what had awoken him, but he was there, awake, staring at the ceiling of the room he was in. He could hear his dad in the next room milling around and he figured he might as well go see what he was up to. He got out of bed and walked across the floor to his mom and dad's room. As he pushed open the door he could see his mother was still in bed and probably still asleep. There was a faint light coming from the bathroom and Michael walked over and whispered, "Dad".

"What are you doing? Why aren't you ready?" His dad opened the door and began the questioning.

"What do you mean?"

"You are going with me, aren't you?" His dad responded.

"You mean you were serious?" Michael said with a very confused expression.

"Yes I was, now go and get dressed we need to get going."

Michael dressed in a hurry and was ready even before his dad had come into the room to get him. They left for the hangar and as he closed the door to the room, Michael had a feeling of uncertainty. He hoped everything was going to be okay and he would see his mother and sisters again. He paused for a moment and then realized that was a silly thought. His dad would never let anything bad happen to him. He had known that for his entire life. Never, had his dad ever put him in danger in anyway and this was no different.

Michael and his dad made their way to the hangar and met the two sergeants there. They were all dressed to go and had made some coffee for them. Michael had never drunk coffee so he just said, "No thanks." His dad immediately got busy going over the plan and he could feel the tension and urgency in the hangar.

"Has Major Daniels reported any movement of our target?" His dad began to question the other two.

"He said everything is the same, no one has moved or left."

Michael and his dad began to do their final dressing and preparation for going outside. Just like before, they had already put on the under clothing of long johns that were heated by a small battery pack. They had also put on the overalls of winter gear. All that was left was for them to put on a heavy coat and mittens and the goggles filled with the warm gel. They also had to put on the radios and microphones again and as they did Michael could hear the conversation between his dad and Major Daniels, who was in the computer room.

"How does it look?" His dad asked.

"It looks good, no movement, and no other targets as of now," Major Daniels responded.

"Good, then we go as soon as we are ready. Make sure you keep an eye on them, we don't need any surprises."

During this conversation the two sergeants had gotten on their snow mobiles and were ready to go. They had armed themselves with some M-16's. Michael just stood and watched as all of this work was going on and he really had no idea what his place in all of this was.

His dad had also taken an M-16 from the case and he carried a 9mm sidearm as well. Michael wasn't offered a gun and he thought that was okay as he probably couldn't shoot it anyway. His dad instructed him on how the snowmobile worked and told Michael to pay attention, "Just in case."

Michael had not been so focused in all of his life on anything. He listened and he understood everything he was being told. He felt a little nervous, but he also had a feeling of excitement. It wasn't everyday a twelve year old got to go on military maneuvers. His dad and the others started their snowmobiles and Michael was instructed to get on the one with his dad. He did and reached his arms around him for safety. He felt good, strong.

The three snowmobiles moved slowly out of the door to the hangar and one of the sergeants turned around and closed the door. It was very dark and very cold outside and Michael heard only his breathing in the radio.

"Let's go!" The command from his dad came on the radio and Michael felt the forward surge of movement.

It was very dark and the snow was very white. Without the light from the moon, which was not shining at this time on the planet, it was hard to see. Michael noticed his dad and the other two were wearing a different type of goggles. He asked what they were and his dad told him they were for night vision. He had heard about them on TV once but didn't know how they worked. He wanted to ask, but the mission was beginning and there wasn't time.

"How do we look Major?" His dad said on the radio.

"Looking good Colonel, you are nine miles from the target."

"Keep me posted on distance, we don't want to get to close and give ourselves away."

Since they were so close to the North Pole, it had been impossible to determine headings of north, south, east, and west, so it was decided to just say right or left or back.

"Go right ten degrees," instructed the Major.

"Right ten, roger," his dad replied.

Michael felt his dad turn and saw the other two follow in line. The path they were on was dimly lit by a head light that put out very little light and Michael felt as if he was traveling in a black hole. He wondered how his dad could even see where they were going. He then realized it might not matter, it wasn't as if they were going to hit anything up here. "Maybe a polar bear," he chuckled to himself.

"You're eight miles and closing, on course." Major Daniels was giving them their progress.

In a distance Michael thought he could see a very dim

light. He squinted a bit, but guessed it was just a reflection of the headlight on the snow flakes up ahead.

Major Daniels continued to count down the distance and heading for them as they sped across the snow and ice. As they got closer to the target, his dad began to slow down. He was making sure that they were not going to be detected. He had told Michael that they needed the element of surprise if this was going to work. He had also told Michael their plan was to capture the people who were shooting at them and then hold them until help could arrive to pick them up.

As they reached a spot four miles from the target, Michael's dad stopped and shut off the light. The other two followed and soon they were sitting in the dark, cold, emptiness of the Arctic.

"How are we doing Major?" His dad asked.

"Right on target Colonel and no one has moved yet."

"Good, we are going to move up to two miles. Let me know if anything moves."

They then started slowly to move without the light. Michael's dad knew they would be spotted from a far distance if the light was on. He had hoped they could get closer without being heard. They continued slowly as Major Daniels read them the distance and heading. It seemed to take a long time to move the two miles and Michael could feel some cold air work its way into his clothing.

As they reached a spot two miles from the target, they could just barely make out a faint light in the distance. They weren't sure what it was, but with the help of the satellite and Major Daniels they soon knew it was what they were after. They were told that was their target. They stopped and shut down the vehicles. There was a deafening silence when they disembarked and stood in the snow and ice looking ahead at the horizon, looking toward the place where they knew was an enemy.

Michael and his dad stood waiting for the other two to catch up. Soon, all four of them were assembled there on the cold, icy, emptiness of the north and gathered their plans.

"Let's take it slow and easy and wait for my signal before anybody moves." His dad's voice was calm and sure.

"You stay with me Michael," his dad said as he grabbed him by the coat.

The four of them began to move toward the faint light. It was hard to walk in the snow and ice but they seemed to be making good time. The boots they were wearing seemed to work very well in this environment. Before they knew it, they were only about two hundred yards from what looked like a big, white tent.

Michael's dad gave the stop sign and they all stopped and crouched down. There was no movement that they could see and for a moment it seemed to be a frozen scene in time. The moment they began to move again a light came on inside the big white tent. At that instant, Major Daniels voice came on the radio and said, "Hold on!"

Michael's dad held up a clenched fist, which was the sign to stop. "What is it?" Michael's dad asked into the radio in a soft voice so he couldn't be heard by anyone else.

"There is something moving toward you from your ten o'clock position. It is moving fast and it is not on the ground... wait... get out of there!"

The four turned and began to run back toward the snowmobiles.

"What do you show on the screen?" Michael's dad said as he breathed hard from running.

Michael was actually in front of the others, he was definitely fast even in the snow and ice. Or was it he was just scared?

"It is a helicopter, and it's heading right for the target area."

"I want to stop and check it out, is it safe to stop here?"

"Yes, it is only about a half mile from you, but it is moving at an angle, not directly over you." Major Daniels voice was broken and a bit hurried as he tried to make sure they were not in danger of being spotted.

They stopped running and laid down in the snow. They were not worried about being spotted on the snow because it was very dark and they were wearing white suits.

From the air it would be impossible to see them. They would blend into the snow and ice on the ground. But their snowmobiles were not hidden and it turned out to be a good thing they left them where they did.

Soon they could hear the chopper blades banging in the frigid air. Then a bright light scanned across the snow and ahead of where they lay. A split second later the chopper roared overhead and off into the night. Michael's dad had looked at it with his night vision binoculars and announced, "It's North Korean."

"It's what?" Major Daniels replied.

"North Korean," his dad repeated.

"Well, what the heck are they doing up here and why are they shooting at us?"

Major Daniels seemed to be a bit annoyed at the news of the helicopter belonging to the North Korean's.

"We're coming back, we need a new plan," his dad said as they stood up to head back to the snowmobiles.

Michael joined with his dad and walked next to him. He was a bit nervous over the whole ordeal and was looking for a little protection. His dad sensed this and put his arm on his shoulder and asked him if he was okay. Michael shook his head yes and was just happy to be going home, or at least back to the camp.

By the time they had made it back to the snowmobiles, Michael was beginning to get cold. They had been outside now for about four hours and it was not a good day to be out doing winter sports, he thought.

They got on the snowmobiles and it was welcomed warmth for Michael to feel the exhaust on his legs. He just sat there for a moment as his dad got ready to go and tried to get as much heat as he could. As they started back toward their camp, Michael was thinking of how lucky they were to not have been spotted by the helicopter. It didn't seem to take as long to get back and soon they were pulling into the hangar. It was well past noon now and everyone was awake and waiting for information on what they had discovered.

Michael was just happy to be where it was warm again and as he removed his goggles, he could see his mother standing in the hangar, and she did not look happy.

"So are you going to tell me who's big idea it was to take my son out in this weather to catch some bad guys with guns?" His mom addressed his dad and sounded a little bit mad.

"There was no big idea, I needed his help and he was there for that reason. We would have completed this mission had it not been for the unexpected visitors." His dad seemed a bit mad as well.

"I'm going to the computer room to see what is going on, I will talk to you in a minute," his dad said as he walked past his mom.

Michael went over to her and gave her a hug. He whispered in her ear, "It's okay mom, I was fine and everything was going good until the helicopter came over."

"What helicopter?" she said as she backed up from Michael.

"There was a helicopter that flew over and landed by the tent with the guys we went after. Dad said it was from North Korea."

Michael's mom just stood for a second with a puzzled look on her face and then she suddenly turned and headed into the complex. Michael finished taking off his heavy coat and radio gear and then followed her into the hallway.

"Where are you going, mom?" He yelled down the hall curiously.

"To see your dad and get some answers!"

Chapter 14

Michael sat across from his dad at the small kitchen table in the room where they were living. His dad was drinking some coffee and Michael was sipping some hot chocolate. It was early in the morning, but you couldn't tell by the sun coming in the window. There was no sun, just darkness outside.

"Why is it so dark all the time up here?" Michael began a conversation.

"Because we are near the top of the world and during these months the sun is too low in the sky to bring light," his dad responded as he looked at Michael.

"Why is that satellite able to see us then?" Michael asked another question.

His dad looked up at him with sort of a gaze and then said, "Do you know what is meant by infrared light?"

Michael then realized he might have gotten himself into one of those lecture sessions that his educated parents liked to do with him. They thought if they returned his question with one of their own he was suppose to learn something from it.

"See Michael, the satellite that is over head in the upper levels of the earth's atmosphere is equipped with a camera that picks up infrared heat, which is heat that we can't see with our eyes. Everyone puts off some heat as we breathe and live. That satellite is able to see our body heat and it shows as an orange or red dot depending on how much heat there is."

"So that satellite way up in space can see a little person's heat on the earth?"

"That's right, and that is what you saw on the computer screen when you saw those orange dots."

"And the bright orange dot with the three around it was a camp fire and three people?"

"Yes, but it probably wasn't actually a camp fire with logs, since it was in a tent it probably was a gas fire like in a portable stove."

"Is that how Major Daniels saw the helicopter?"

"Yeah, he would have picked up the heat from the engine exhaust on the chopper and then he identified it using the computer image."

"Wow, this is interesting," Michael was enjoying this conversation with his dad. He was beginning to understand more of what was going on. He decided to continue with some unanswered questions.

"What did you tell mom about me going with you?"

"I explained to her that you had gone with me to help me with spotting the enemy and with getting them back to our camp if we captured them. I told her you were never in danger and I needed the extra man."

"Did she buy it?"

"I think so, but there really wasn't anything to buy," his dad looked at him with a smile.

"You are an important part of this mission, Michael. I brought you up here so you could help me, I am not going to leave you here when I need you out there," his dad said as he pointed to the outside.

"So why are we really up here?" Michael decided to go for the long shot on this one. He didn't think there was some ulterior motive for him being here, but he just thought he would ask anyway. He knew it wasn't everyday that families went to live in the extreme environment of the Arctic.

"Why do you ask that Buddy?" His dad responded with a kind of puzzled look.

"I don't know, I just think it was kind of silly to put a place like this in the middle of the Arctic Circle just to study something that I don't even understand."

"Michael, do you even know what I do for a living?"

"Yeah, you're a school teacher, right?"

"I am more than that Bud, I am in charge of a department for the government that puts satellites into outer space. We moved to where we live now because I got moved up in the department and became the head man."

"So what's the big deal, you've been in charge before."

"This is different, you don't know the whole story of what I do and I'm sure your mom has never told you. It isn't a secret, but there are times when I can't talk about it. This time was different because it wasn't a secret and I was able to bring you guys up here with me so we could be together and see this place. I don't think anyone in your class could say they went on 'vacation' to the Arctic."

"This doesn't seem like a 'vacation' to me."

"Figure of speech, didn't you learn that in school?"

"Yeah, it's called an idiom or idiot or something like that."

"There are times when you really amaze me Bud, this isn't one of them."

"Well I don't know, I try and it seems so hard for me," Michael was beginning to sound a little defeated by the whole thing and his dad recognized that.

"Michael, it isn't that hard, it's actually easy if you just put your mind to it."

"I try to and it seems no matter what I do I always fail."

"You haven't failed up here, actually you had the best idea of anyone when you said we should use the satellite to find those people."

"But you and mom are always on my back about school and everything."

"That's our job, that's why we have children, so we can make them do the things we want."

"Are you trying to be funny?"

"Yes. We just want you to succeed, to do better than we have and make a good life for yourself. Your mom and I just want you to be happy and that is why we push you so hard. Someday you will understand this, someday when you have children."

Michael got up and filled his cup with some more hot chocolate that was on the stove. His dad asked him to bring the coffee and he did. As he sat back down, he continued to ask some questions he wanted answered.

"Dad, why are there other people shooting at us?"

"I'm not sure Michael, but you can bet we will find out."

121

"I heard you say they were from Korea?"

"Actually it is North Korea. That is what I saw on the side of the chopper when it flew over us out on the ice."

"Why would someone from there be up here and shooting at us?"

"Well you see Michael, some countries don't like the United States. They try and hurt us with whatever they can. You remember the terrorist attacks when you were in the third or fourth grade?"

"Not really, I don't pay too much attention to the news like you and mom do."

"Maybe you will now, huh?"

"Are you being funny again?"

"No"

"Well what are we going to do? Did you and the others come up with a new plan?"

"Actually we have. I put a call into Washington on the satellite phone and they are checking into why there is a small group from North Korea up here. They probably won't have an answer for a while, so we came up with a contingency plan just in case. It appears to us that there are only three people living in a large tent about ten miles from here. But you already knew about them didn't you?" His dad was seeing if Michael was paying attention.

"Yeah."

"We do not know how they got here or why. What bothers me is that no one was aware of what we have up here and as far as our government knew, no one cared."

"So why would they just shoot at us for no reason?"

"I think we figured that out as well. See there is a large antennae right above where we were standing when the shots were fired. I think they didn't see us and were shooting at the antennae. I think they were trying to damage the antennae so it wouldn't work. Actually I don't think they know there were even any people up here."

"You mean that they think this place is empty and no one is living here?"

"That is what we think. No one would want to start a war over a few people in the Arctic."

"How would that start a war?"

"If anyone should attack us up here and our government thought it was unjustified, we could attack back and then we end up in a war."

"This all seems to be so complicated. Why can't we just go and talk to them and ask them to stop shooting at us?"

"You really amaze me sometimes Michael. It is just too bad not everyone saw things the way you do. It would be really easy to do that, but we can't."

"Why not?"

"That I cannot tell you. These people may want to hurt us and by just walking up to them may lead us into a problem. Also, I'm not sure if we could even communicate with them enough to find out."

Michael started to think that there was more to what was going on here than he knew about. But he was just not really old enough to understand or care. He just went on to a new question.

"So what's the plan?"

"We are going to go back to that target location with the three in the tent. We are going to see if we can find out what they are doing here and why they are shooting at this installation."

"Isn't that my idea?"

"Right, that is why I said you amaze me sometimes. You already knew what we were planning on doing."

Michael got a big smile on his face. He suddenly had a feeling of smartness. He knew he had special talents and now he had proven it.

Michael and his dad had been sitting and talking for almost an hour now and everyone was beginning to wake up and come into the room where they were.

"We'll talk later Bud, let's get ready for the day." His dad ended the conversation to welcome his sisters to breakfast.

For the first time in his life Michael was beginning to understand some of the things that were going on around him. For the first time he had realized that there was something he was missing in his life. He started to see the light at the end of the tunnel. His dad had talked with him a lot in the past, but this time was different. He was talking to him like he was a man… or a young man. All of the things he had done up here with his dad, he never had done before. Was he actually growing up?

Suddenly there was a knock on the door and Michael announced that he would get it. He opened the door and Major Daniels was standing there.

"Is your dad awake?"

"Yeah, come on in," Michael stepped back to allow him access to their room.

"Dad, there is someone here to see you," Michael said as if he was letting a stranger in the room.

"Be right there," his dad returned a yell.

"How have you been doing Michael?" Major Daniels began a conversation with Michael as he waited.

"Okay, I just want to go back outside and have some fun."

"You will, we are a long way from being finished here."

Michael turned and saw his dad come from his room and he greeted Major Daniels and took over the conversation from Michael.

"What's up?"

"We have a call from Washington in the computer room."

"Well then let's go. Michael, tell your mom I had to go and I'll be back in a while." His dad turned and left the room.

Michael nodded his head and closed the door as the two exited and headed down the hall toward the computer room.

They got to the room in just a few seconds and on the satellite phone and video was one of the commanders of the unit that was running the satellite communications in the Arctic. His name was General Thompson, and he was a friend of Michael's dad. They had served together in the Air Force a couple of times. The introduction was short and then the General told them some of the things he had found out.

"The North Korean's are denying any participation in the Arctic. They said no one from their country to their knowledge was up there."

"So I guess I was wrong in identifying the helicopter?" Colonel Rossi said with a disgusted voice.

"No Colonel, I'm sure you were right. They just won't admit to any wrong doing."

"So what are our options at this point?"

"Well, it would be almost impossible to get you any help at this time. We are a little short handed on troops that can deploy to the Arctic. We really never considered this to be a problem we would have to deal with."

"Neither did I," Colonel Rossi said with a sigh.

"Our intelligence is telling us that it is possible the North Korean's think we are building a space system to spy on them. If that is the case they may try to take it out."

"That is not the news I was hoping for General."

"Sorry about that Mark, but that is all the news I have for now."

"General, I can take care of this with my people up here. I just need to know if I have permission to do it."

"You have permission to do whatever you need to insure the safety of this mission. I don't want to regret letting you take your family with you."

"General, my family is safe and secure. Besides, it was my idea. I would never hold you responsible for this."

"That is why I trust you Mark. Do what you have to and I will send help as soon as we can get it."

"Thank you General and we will be in touch."

Colonel Rossi hung up the phone and turned and looked at Major Daniels, "We have some work to do, get the others, and let's get started."

Chapter 15

THROUGHOUT THE rest of the day, Michael spent his time helping his mother with the cleaning of the room and running back and forth for his dad. He wasn't sure, but he thought it must be a Sunday since he didn't have to attend school. His sisters were spending all of their time watching TV and eating whatever they could find. Every once in a while he would stop to criticize them only to have his mother yell at him. For a while, unless he looked outside, it felt like any Sunday back home.

As the day came to an end, he was anxious for his dad to get back to the room and let him in on the plan. It was late, well past eleven at night before his dad came back. Michael was tired from being up so early in the morning and he had fallen asleep. He slept very well that night, dreaming of running in the snow and riding on snowmobiles. He also had a very strange dream right before he woke up. He was standing on the side of a lake and in the middle was a tent that was on fire. He couldn't figure it out, why would he dream of a tent on a lake? And why would it be on fire?

He woke up to the sound of a knock on the door. Before he could move his dad had opened it and let someone in. He stirred in his bed and then fell back to sleep. The next thing he remembered was his sister, Michelle, pushing on him to wake up and saying something about going to school. "Oh no, not school again, why? I was having so much fun sleeping."

He soon found himself in the big room with the other kids and his mother was starting to show them what they were going to be doing. He raised his hand and his mother asked him what he wanted.

"Why are we in school when there is a problem going on with our safety?"

His mother seemed a little bit upset that Michael had brought that up in front of the other children. She told him to just sit down and be quiet and she would deal with him later. Michael had no idea he had done something wrong.

For most of the day, all Michael did was day dream. He noticed his dad and the other men going back and forth a few times, but couldn't figure out what was going on. As the school day ended and the kids dispersed to their living quarters, Michael just sat in the chair he had been in all day and stared blankly into space. His mother came over to him and nudged him to wake him up.

"What are you doing?" she asked him.

"I'm just thinking," he replied.

"About what?"

"About why we came here and why I am still in this room and not out helping dad."

"You know Michael, your dad does need your help, but right now he just needs time to get his thoughts straight.

He has a great responsibility to the safety of this whole group, as well as you."

"I know that mom, I just want to go help out and that is why I asked the question you didn't answer earlier."

"The reason I didn't answer that question is the other children do not know what is going on and you don't need to tell them. You will frighten them. We have to be absolutely sure we know what is happening before we say it."

"But…"

"No buts Michael, think before you speak!"

Michael just sat there and listened to his mother and wasn't sure why he felt like he was making her mad.

"I'm going to our room, are you coming?" She said as she turned to leave.

"I'll be there in a minute," he replied.

She left the room and Michael continued to sit and think. As he did he noticed his dad come in from the side that led into the hangar.

"Good, I'm glad your still here," he said to Michael.

"Yea I was just waiting to see if you have a plan and how I can help," Michael said to his dad as he came over to him.

"As a matter of fact, I do have a new plan, and you can help."

"Really, what can I do?"

"First you can start by following me into the hangar."

Michael jumped up like he was sitting on a spring, and followed his dad to the airplane hangar. It was a few degrees colder in the hangar because of its size, so he grabbed his sweater on the way out of the room.

"Why are we going in here dad?" Michael asked as they entered.

"Because I need to teach you some things before you can really help me."

"Oh no, not more school," Michael replied.

"Yes more school, but I think you will like this one."

As they entered, Michael could see the other men from the group standing by the airplane looking at some weapons. One of the sergeants that Michael remembered was called 'Soup' came over and welcomed Michael to the group. He asked Michael if he had ever shot a weapon before. He knew the answer because Michael's dad had told him, but he wanted Michael to say it himself.

"Only at the arcades and it was a BB gun," Michael said.

"Good then we have a place to start," Sergeant Campbell said.

Sergeant Campbell was Air Force Special Operations. He was sent on this trip in case his skills were needed. As it turns out, they were. Michael was continuing to understand more about each person's job and why they were sent here.

Michael's dad began to explain to Michael that he would need to learn the basics of firing the M-16 if he was going to be part of the new plan. He probably wouldn't have to, but just in case he needed to know.

Michael was very excited about this. He loved to shoot the guns at the arcades and he had always dreamed of having his own one day. Michael's dad turned and left the hangar and for the next hour Michael received a crash course on a military weapon.

Sergeant Campbell showed Michael how to load it and how to chamber a round. He went over the safety features of the weapon and how to hold it properly and safely. All Michael could think of was, "When do I get to shoot it?"

When the hour was over, Michaels dad came back and asked, "How did he do?"

"Great, he's a natural!" Sergeant Campbell exclaimed.

"Good, now you are officially part of the plan." Michael's dad had a big smile on his face as he announced that. Michael could tell he was proud of him and it made him feel good.

The two of them left to go back to their room. On the way there, Michael and his dad joked and made fun of some things they found funny that no one else would. Like pretending to punch each other and making noises.

They burst through the door and into the room. The rest of the family was sitting on a couch reading a book that Michelle had and they nearly jumped out of their seats as the two came crashing in.

"Family meeting!" Michael's dad announced.

"We're all here what do you want?" His mother said in a disgusted voice.

"It has been decided, by me, that everyone is just going to eat in their own rooms tonight. We, or should I say I, think we should just spend some quiet time together."

Michael's mother was making a gagging sound at the comment. "We spend too much quiet time, what's the real reason?" She asked.

"I think it would just be better if we didn't meet in a big group tonight." As Michael's dad said this, he looked directly at his wife and was making a strange face. No one notice it but his mom and she immediately said it was a great idea. She knew that he was trying to make it not sound like a problem that they shouldn't all be in the same room until they figure out what to do with the enemy so close.

"So what do we want?"

"Mexican!" This was his mother's standard answer for dinner.

Michael could only figure it was from her upbringing in the desert southwest, that she always said Mexican food. He knew it was her favorite, but he really didn't like it so much. He liked Italian.

"Small problem with that," his dad said. "We only have frozen chicken."

"Let's order pizza!" His mother continued to seem like she was having a good time making everyone crazy with her requests.

"I don't think they can get here in thirty minutes," his dad was now in the game. The game was to see if they could agitate the children.

"I want McDonalds," Michelle added. Now it was her turn to get on Michael's nerves.

Michael began to wonder why he wasn't in this game of picking what they would eat. Then he realized they were all joking. How would they get pizza or McDonalds way up here in the middle of nowhere? He figured his mind was only on the new knowledge he had and the fact that he was part of this new plan his dad had. He just wasn't concerned about dinner.

They decided on chicken. They cooked it in the microwave and ate. Then sat as a family and watched a movie on DVD. It was kind of nice to have some time together. They hadn't spent much time in the first couple of days they were here. It seemed like so much was going on there wasn't any time to just sit and relax. They had been there for a total of five days and this was actually the first time they had been able to sit and watch TV and just talk.

Michael's dad had kind of a restless mood about him most of the time, but he did a good job of hiding it. Michael knew something was up, but his mother had made it clear not to say anything in front of the other kids. Therefore, he just sat quietly and watched the movie.

As night fell, all of the kids became very tired and began falling asleep. Even Michael was finding it hard to stay awake and just let sleep come. His mom and dad took them to their beds and said goodnight.

Chapter 16

THE NEXT morning around six thirty, the room was lit by the light coming through the door. Michael opened his eyes to see his dad come into the room.

"Are you awake?" He asked Michael.

"Yeah, what do you want?"

"Get up and come with me."

His dad turned and left the room. Michael rolled out of bed and got dressed. He usually wouldn't move this fast, but he sensed something was going on. He stopped to use the bathroom and quickly brushed his teeth, then made his way into the kitchen area.

"Dad, it's really early what are we doing?"

"We have to move up our plans. I was planning on going after these people late this evening, but we just got some new information and we need to act."

What Michael didn't know was that early this morning a call came in from Washington. General Thompson had informed his dad that a CIA man had confirmed that the North Korean's were planning on destroying the base in the Arctic. The supply helicopter that they saw that day on the ice was bringing in explosives and they were going to be acting soon. Michael's dad now had an urgency to act first, so he moved up the plan immediately.

General Thompson told him that they were assembling a team to assist them, but it was going to be at least twenty-four hours before they could get there. Therefore, the decision was made for the group in the Arctic to make a move and try to stop the attack.

Michael followed his dad out of the room and down the hall. His dad kept asking him questions about if he was comfortable with the M-16 and if he thought he could drive the snowmobile. Michael was a little bit confused, but he felt like he knew what he was doing after his training session with the sergeant. His dad told him several times that he had confidence in him and he knew he would do well.

As they entered the hangar, the other men were all assembled and this time Major Daniels was there as well. Michael asked who was on the computer and his dad told him that Mr. Franks was in the control room with the satellite and would be doing the direction from there. His dad also made it clear that they needed every available man and that was why Major Daniels was going, as well as Michael.

Just like before they dressed in their winter gear and put on the radio receivers and microphones. Almost immediately Michael could feel himself warm up and could here his breathing in the car piece.

"Let's do a radio check," his dad announced and each man said check.

"Michael you ride with me, Major Daniels is taking one snowmobile and the sergeants are taking the others. I just wish we had more snowmobiles and men, but we must make do with what we have."

"Roger," Major Daniels replied.

They pulled the snowmobiles out of the hangar and closed the door behind them. It felt like Michael had done this before. It was just like the last time. It was cold and dark and a little bit scary, like the haunted house at Halloween.

Michael got on board with his dad and they began to pull away. As they did, Michael's dad checked with Mr. Franks to make sure all was well and he said it was. "Target is stable and not moving."

They sped off across the frozen landscape with the hope that this was going to work. Michael's dad had the confidence it would and Michael knew again that his dad would not put him in danger. He felt good about this and also knew if he needed, he could handle the weapon that was on his snowmobile.

As the distance to the target began to get shorter, they went into the stealth mode again. They turned off the lights and pulled back on the throttle to a coast. At two miles away, they stopped and joined up on the ice for a last minute check and direction before heading to the final target. Michael's dad handed him an M-16 and made sure he knew how to take off the safety.

"Only if I tell you too or you are in danger," his dad made it clear not to aim or shoot without permission from him.

Michael was getting nervous. He's only still a boy. He then for some reason remembered the stories of the young boys who fought in the Revolutionary War. How they were only ten or eleven. They fought and did a good job, so why couldn't he. He was trying to build up his nerve, but once again he reminded himself that his dad would not put him in danger.

As they got closer, he could see the outline of the white tent against the dark background. His dad told them to stop. They did and then he ordered the others to take up positions around the tent. Major Daniels and the two sergeants then went to different points around the tent. Michael and his dad were directly in front of the tent door or flap and he could just barely see Major Daniels to their right. The one sergeant was to the left and he guessed the other one must be around back. They were about fifty feet from the tent and he could see the glow of a fire inside. Other than that there was no movement.

Mr. Franks confirmed, "There are three bodies in the tent and they are not moving. Probably still asleep," he added.

"Good," replied Michael's dad.

Major Daniels now confirmed he was in position and then Sergeant Campbell confirmed his position.

"Sergeant Banks are you in position?" His dad asked.

"In ten seconds," came the reply.

Michael's dad told Michael in a soft and confident voice, "You stay here, and I am going up to the tent. Do not move. You are my backup if someone comes this way. If you have to, just take off the safety and point and shoot, but make sure you do not... shoot... me!"

Michael nodded his head yes. He wanted to say something, but his mouth wouldn't work. He was actually a bit scared and excited at the same time. He removed his mitten glove and only had his regular glove with the fingers in it. He needed his finger to pull the trigger and it wouldn't work in the mitten. Almost as soon as he did this, his hand started to get cold. He ignored it because his adrenaline was working now.

Michael kneeled down on his right knee and rested the gun across his leg. He practiced lifting into position a couple of times and was rehearsing what he should do in case he needed to fire. His hand was on the trigger area and his thumb was ready to click the gun off of safe and into fire mode.

His dad slowly made his way to the front of the tent. As he did, Michael could see something move inside the tent. It was a shadow on the tent of someone standing. He wasn't sure if his dad could see it because he was so close and he kept moving toward it.

He tried to warn him with the radio, but for some reason his wasn't working. He picked up some snow to throw and get his attention, but it was so cold it was like powder. He was left with a decision. He had to warn his dad someone was moving.

He put the gun back on his shoulder, stood up, and began to move toward the tent. He could see his dad right next to the tent flap and he guessed he was going to enter it and take them by surprise. As he moved he saw the others closing in around the tent. It was now or never, so he began to run. As he got by the tent, he tripped on something and his dad jerked around to see what the noise was. When he did he saw Michael falling into the snow right at the edge of the tent. He had tripped over one of the lines holding up the tent and he had broken it loose. This began to cause a chain reaction of events that was hard to understand and believe for all of them.

Michael's dad looked at him, looked at the line, looked at him, and then to the tent.

All of the sudden the tent began to collapse. The wind was blowing the sides up and around, and as it did, it was breaking the lines loose that held it down. The front of the tent was caught by the wind and lifted up. Right there in front of them were several boxes marked Explosives. Just past them in the tent they could see a man standing in boots and a coat looking directly at them. Michael's dad raised his gun and pointed it at the man, but he seemed to not notice them. At that point Michael could see why he was frozen in his boots. He was looking at what was happening to the tent. The tent had begun to fall apart and some of the material fell directly onto the stove with the flame in it. It caught fire instantaneously and began to spread fast. Michael heard some yelling and then saw the man turn and run and the other two in the tent followed.

At that point Michael's dad saw this and ordered a retreat. He yelled into the radio, "Get Back!"

Michael stood frozen in his tracks, not able to move for some reason.

His dad grabbed Michael by the coat and began dragging him away from the tent through the ice and snow. Michael could see the fire spread. He was looking back toward the tent as he felt himself being pulled over the ice by his dad. He could see the boxes marked explosives and then in an instant saw the flames reach them. A huge fire ball erupted from the tent and he felt the concussion of a very large explosion. The fire had made its way to the boxes of explosives and set them off

The last thing he remembered was his dad throwing him

down and jumping on him. He wasn't sure at this point what had happened. Only that he was on the ground and having trouble breathing. Then silence.

Chapter 17

THERE WAS no sound, just empty air. Then the silence was broken by Mr. Franks, yelling into the radio, "What was that? My whole screen just lit up! Are you guys okay?"

Michael could hear him, but he could not speak.

Nothing.

Then a faint voice could be heard. It was scrambled in static and he could not make out who or what it was.

"Come back, over!" Michael was struggling to speak and he said what he had been told to say, if he didn't understand someone.

Still just static.

In the control room, Mr. Franks was becoming concerned. Could something have gone wrong? Could the mission have failed? Are they all dead? The questions seemed to pierce his brain and no one could answer them.

Back on the ice, Michael laid motionless on the ground under his dad. He could feel his dad breathing, but he was not awake. The blast must have knocked him out. Michael tried to move, but he was having a hard time in all of the clothes he was wearing and the weight of his dad. Then he felt his dad move.

"Dad," Michael said into the microphone. But he did not hear it in his ear. He guessed his radio wasn't working, so he yelled it.

"Dad, are you okay!?"

"I think so, are you?" Words from Michael's dad meant he was alive and okay. Michael felt a great joy in this and then he felt his dad move off of him. As he sat up, he could see a huge hole in the ice where the tent was and a small amount of flame burning out the last of the fuel and material. There seemed to be an eerie silence to the whole scene.

His dad sat up and shook his head clear. "What happened?"

Michael said, "Don't you remember, the tent caught on fire and the explosives blew up!"

"Oh yeah, now it is coming clear. Where are the others and the people who were in the tent?"

Michael did not know and he told his dad he didn't think their radios were working. His dad reached inside his coat and started to try to adjust the radio and was saying things into his microphone, but all Michael could hear was static.

"The blast must have knocked them out," his dad surmised.

"Well, what do we do?" Michael asked. He was beginning to feel the cold and he was sure the others were too. He stood up and looked around. All he could see was white snow and black air. His dad stood next to him and began to mess with the radio again, and almost as if standing up fixed the radio, he could hear his voice in the ear piece and Michael could as well.

"Major Daniels are you there? His dad said.

"I'm here Colonel where were you?" Major Daniels replied.

"Radio was out. Are you okay?"

"I'm fine, what the heck happened?"

"The fire got to the explosives and set them off. Are Sergeants Banks and Campbell with you?"

"Colonel we are about one click west or to your left from you." Sergeant Campbell came on the radio with the news."

"Are you guys okay?"

"Yes, and we have some good news. We captured the enemy, they ran right into us when the tent exploded and we got them!"

It was easy to hear the excitement in his voice. He continued to explain the situation, "When the tent caught fire they ran out of it and in a panic left everything behind. As they ran away they ran directly into Sergeant Banks and me."

"That is great news sergeant, we will be right there!" Michael's dad was also sounding excited. They were able to capture these guys and no one was hurt, at least not bad. The concussion from the explosion rocked them a bit, but no one was injured.

Within a few minutes Michael, his dad, and Major Daniels were able to locate the others and join up with them. When they got there they greeted each other with a lot of smiles and thankfulness that everyone was okay. Major Daniels put his arm around Michael and gave him a big hug and said, "Way to go big boy!"

Michael felt proud. He wasn't sure if he did anything great, but he felt proud to be a part of this.

Mr. Franks' voice was heard on the radio, "Come in Colonel, are you okay?"

"We're fine, we just lost radio contact for a minute."

"What happened?"

"We had an explosion, but everyone is alright and we are on our way back."

"Thank goodness, I lost computer images of your location, so you're on your own. Do you know the way back?"

"Roger, we will be okay, we can follow our tracks back."

The three Korean's were standing there with guns pointed at them. They were shivering from the cold and had a very frightened look on their faces. It was if they had never seen a human before. Michael's dad said that proved they did not know anyone was up here, because of how surprised they looked.

They began the walk back to the snowmobiles. The wind was blowing and it made it hard to move forward. The three enemy soldiers were beginning to show signs of freezing, but there was nothing they could do for them. Michael's dad gave one his outer parka to help him stay warm and the Major and one of the sergeants did the same. It was a very nice gesture Michael thought. But, that is one of the things he learned about Americans. No matter what the situation, we are always ready to help someone, even if they meant to harm us.

They continued to plod through the snow and ice on the way to the snowmobiles. They were following their tracks that were left when they first arrived. Michael thought that it must be like walking on the moon. It was if the snow was permanently frozen with the imprint of their shoes.

When they reached the snowmobiles Michael's dad took some zip ties out of a bag and put them around the wrists of the enemy soldiers. That was done so they could not do anything while being transported back to the base. Michael told everyone he didn't think it was really necessary since if they tried to escape they were sure to freeze to death in the Arctic. "But it was done just in case and for safety." His dad told him.

They got on board, Michael again rode with his dad and one Korean soldier got on each of the other snowmobiles. The men then put a blanket around them and secured it to them so it wouldn't blow off on the trip. The blankets were from a survival kit on the snowmobiles. When they did this all three soldiers smiled at Michael and the others as if they were happy to be covered and protected from the cold.

They turned toward the base and accelerated into the cold darkness. Michael could feel some heat from the engine, but he was really getting cold. They had been on the ice for several hours and even with the best clothing it was cold.

The wind was howling through Michael's head and the piercing cold was biting into him. He could only image how the Koreans must feel, they were not as well protected from the cold. The trip back was hard and it was a welcome site when the base came into view in the distance as they sped across the ice.

As they approached the hangar the others were prepared for them and had already opened the doors. They drove the snowmobiles right in and the doors were closed behind them. All of the men dismounted the snowmobiles and started to shake off the cold. The three Korean soldiers just sat frozen to the seats. They were half afraid to move and half frozen in place. No one spoke Korean, so they had to rely on gestures to get them to do anything.

Mr. Franks came running into the hangar to greet them along with some of the children. Michael's mother was already there, she was the one who had opened the doors. Mr. Franks had informed her of the events so far and she was very anxious to see that her two men where okay.

She gave Michael a huge hug and then kind of glared at her husband. She was just not happy that he had taken her only son into the danger zone. He smiled back at her not sure if he was really in trouble or not.

They escorted the Korean soldiers into a tool cage that was in the hangar. It was the only place in the building that had a lock on it. There was no way they could let them loose in the base and the cage was the only alternative.

Major Daniels suggested that someone go get something hot for them and several of the other mother's who were with them were already doing that. They came into the hangar carrying coffee and some hot chocolate. They offered some to the Koreans and they gladly accepted. They were smiling as they sipped it. Mr. Franks was informing Michael's dad of the news that General Thompson had called when they were on the ice. The Special Forces team was en route and would take control of the prisoners when they arrived in about eight hours. Michael's dad was glad to hear that since he wasn't really thrilled about having three more people to be responsible for and also worry about.

He turned to Michael and said, "Why were you running towards me?"

Michael responded, "To warn you that they were moving in the tent."

"What did you do to fall on the tent?" His dad was asking as they began to get out of their winter clothes. The others in the hangar were all listening very intently. Everyone wanted to know what had happened.

"I tripped over the rope that was holding up the tent and it broke off the ground. Then the tent started to fall down and that is when you saw me and the men inside."

"Well how did it catch fire?" His dad continued to ask questions as if he hadn't been there.

"When the tent fell, it fell on the flame in the middle and caught fire and it spread to the explosives."

"I'm starting to recall this now," his dad said as he seemed to shake out the haze in his mind.

Major Daniels then stepped up and said, "That is when you ordered a retreat and we all turned and ran away from the tent. The next thing I knew it exploded. The explosion knocked me down."

"What explosion?!" Michael's mother asked as she moved into the group.

"The tent had explosives in it and the fire set them off," Michael continued to explain.

"And where were you and your father?"

"Running, or actually dad was running and dragging me away, and then when I saw it explode he threw me down and jumped on me."

His mother turned and looked at his dad, the others began to back away fearing the worst. Instead she just said, "You are so lucky he didn't get hurt."

"I think we are all lucky no one got hurt and we accomplished what we set out to do, thanks to Michael." His dad had walked over and put his arm around Michael's shoulder.

Everyone had heard the story and even Michelle had a nice thing to say to Michael as they began to exit the hangar and head into the living area. As she walked by Michael, Michelle whispered, "Way to go big brother, you didn't mess it up like I thought you would."

It was at that point Michael realized his clumsiness was really what had saved the day. Just like he thought when he was outside the first time and he looked back through the window at the faces of these people. "I saved them and maybe the world," he thought to himself.

He looked around and was surprised to find he was the only one left in the hangar besides the three Korean soldiers and Sergeant Banks, who was guarding them. They had been given some food and some more coffee and a couple more blankets and it looked like they were very happy to be safe and warm. They did have a strange look on their faces and kept whispering to each other in Korean.

Sergeant Banks told Michael he thinks they were surprised that the buildings they were shooting at had people in them. He chuckled a bit and then said, "I bet they can't believe that we are living here."

Michael laughed in response to the comment, but he really didn't see any humor in any of this. These people were going to blow this place up and kill all of them. He then turned and left the hangar. As he walked into the main building, he started to think how lucky they all were. He also started to feel something else. Was it pride, courage, he wasn't sure. All he knew was that he had done it! "I went out into the Arctic and saved the world!" He smiled and walked off toward his room.

Chapter 18

Michael was sitting with his dad in the computer room when the call came in from the Special Forces team. They were on final approach to the base in helicopters that had launched from an aircraft carrier near the edge of the Polar Cap. They had refueled en route and were planning on landing, picking up the prisoners, and then departing immediately. There was no need for them to stay since Michael had taken care of capturing the enemy. At least that is the story he planned on telling his friends when he got home.

His dad got up and left the room. Michael assumed he was on his way to meet the team that was coming in. Michael also got up and decided he would go back to his room. He was feeling tired from the long day and wanted to just lie down for a while.

Back in the hangar the Colonel and the others where getting ready to welcome the Special Forces team. They had gotten into their winter gear and were ready to open the doors. After a short wait, the call came in on the radio that they were on the ground. Michael's dad opened the door and immediately saw the soldiers heading toward them. As they entered, the lead man gave a salute to the Colonel and then shook his hand. Colonel Rossi returned the salute and shake and then said, "Glad to see you guys."

The leader of the team was a Captain and he was dressed in all white as was his team. The entered the hangar and then Major Daniels closed the doors. The helicopters that brought them were in the area near the hangar, the pilots had kept them running so they would stay warm.

"We don't have a lot of time so let's get to it," the Captain said.

"Right," Colonel Rossi returned with a nod.

"The three Koreans are in the cage. They were sleeping when we surprised them and they had not dressed properly to be outside up here."

"Right, we have a suit they can put on and then we will take them to the helo's." The captain directed his men to the cage and they began the task of readying the prisoners for transport.

As they did the Captain was beginning to talk to Colonel Rossi about what had happened. He told the Colonel that they had gotten a call that the base in the Arctic was in danger and had left their station in Great Britain. He continued to explain that they had actually been transported to a British Carrier off the coast of Greenland. From there they steamed to the edge of the Polar Cap and took helicopters the rest of the way.

They had made it to the base in less than eight hours. The captain said he was sorry they didn't get there sooner, but they just could not move any faster. Colonel Rossi explained how they were able to capture the enemy without a shot being fired and the part Michael played in all of it.

It wasn't long, maybe a couple of minutes, and they were all ready to move out. The Colonel opened the hangar doors and said goodbye to the Captain. The team moved the prisoners out of the hangar and made their way towards the helicopters. The Colonel, Major, two Sergeants, and now Michael who had joined them, stood and watched as the helicopters took off and headed south toward the ship that was waiting.

Michael said to his dad as they watched the choppers take off, "What is going to happen to them now?"

His dad was talking loudly over the roar of the choppers and said, "They are going to be questioned and then probably returned to their country." He looked a bit puzzled at Michael, wondering where he had come from. The last he knew Michael had gone to the room to rest.

As they made there way back into the hangar and closed the doors Michael's dad asked, "What are you doing Bud? I thought you went to lie down."

"I did but I wanted to see what was happening. I wanted to see if you needed my help."

His dad smiled and looked at the others that were listening to the conversation. He then said, "He cracks me up…, do we need his help? What a character."

They all laughed and made their way back into the living area of the base. It was late in the evening and everyone was very tired from such a long day. As they entered the great room they saw all of the others, women, men, and children working in the kitchen area.

"What's going on?" Michael's dad asked.

"We're making a dinner for everyone to celebrate," his mom replied.

"That's great, we should celebrate. We did some good work today and Michael is the hero."

Michael didn't know what to do. He had never been a hero before. Should he make a speech or something? He just laughed and went over and sat on a chair in the corner. He was just hoping it wasn't his turn to clean up.

When dinner was ready they all gathered around the big table and began to eat. It was a fun dinner, everyone was in a good mood including Michael's mother. He wasn't sure if she was happy about him being so close to danger, but she seemed okay with it now.

After the dinner was over, Michael's dad stood up and asked for everyone's attention. He began to explain some of the events of the day. He told them about what had happened on the ice and how Michael had saved the day with his act of heroics in collapsing the tent and forcing the soldiers into the frozen world and right into the Sergeants who took them captive. Everyone applauded Michael and the two Sergeants as they stood up to take a bow, half in fun and half out of respect for how the others were treating them. Michael had a huge smile on his face. He had never been applauded before.

Finally, the day was over and the families were back in their rooms for the first night without a problem. Michael and Michelle played a video game while Kimberly just sat and watched intently. His parents sat on the couch and talked about the events and how happy they were that everyone was now safe. Every once in a while, Michael would look over to his parents and smile. He seemed different now, he had more of a confident air about him and he wasn't arguing with his sister as much as he used to.

His dad leaned over a little closer to his mother and whispered, "He has really grown up in a short time, hasn't he?"

His mother nodded her head and smiled at Michael. Maybe what had happened, as dangerous as she thought it was, was actually a good thing for Michael to have experienced. This however, did not negate how much trouble Michael's dad was going to be in when they got home.

The day ended and everyone went to sleep. Right before Michael fell asleep, he remembered the dream he had the other night. The one he had of the tent on the lake, on fire. Kind of weird he thought... that is almost exactly what happened.

The next morning it was business as usual or business the way it was suppose to be. Nothing on this trip was usual so far. The kids all went to class with Michael's mother and the adults all went to work setting up the laboratory. It seemed like sort of a boring schedule, except that the activities were all taking place on the frozen ice of the North Pole, like that could really be boring!

At the end of the day, they all met for dinner and it was nice to sit and eat without the worry of being shot at. The next several weeks continued the same way. They would do their job and then meet for an informal dinner and discuss what was going on and enjoy each others company. The kids liked to play together and had started several games using the items in the room. One game had them playing swordsman using the long empty paper rolls from the computers as swords. The adults didn't mind as long as no one got hurt. Michael sometimes would just sit and watch the kids. He seemed to start feeling like he was getting too old for silly games. Even the young man who was about Michael's age had started to follow Michael's lead and not play with the younger ones. Michael couldn't believe he may actually have started to become a role model.

It was fun though, and Michael was finally enjoying this adventure the way he had thought he would. He even enjoyed attending school with his mother. She was easy on him and let him work at his pace. She treated him like a big boy and he liked that. He started to help the younger children in the group with math and reading. She was very surprised by this, since he had always hated to help anyone with school work. He became like a second teacher, taking a small group of the little kids and reading with them. He even had Kimberly with him at times and let her read and do the activities with the others.

There even came a day when he said to his mother, "I like school, we are really having fun and learning too!"

She of course was shocked by this outburst. Michael had never said he liked school before.

Michael's dad was in and out of the room several times a day. Checking on the kids and saying how happy he was to have his family with him. He took Michael with him a few times outside to do work on the outside of the buildings. Michael really enjoyed this, it gave him a chance to explore and learn about the Arctic.

He learned so much in a short time. Like how cold it really was up there. He commented once to his dad, "Hard to believe that it can be so cold here and so warm in other places."

His dad took that opportunity for a geography lesson and Michael actually understood the earth's curvature and lines of latitude that his dad was explaining to him. At one point he actually thought that he couldn't wait to get back to his regular school so he could share all of his new knowledge with his friends.

He also thought how cool it would be to actually know about places where no one else had been. He thought about the report he could write for his Social Studies teacher, Mrs. Robinson, and how she would be impressed with all of his knowledge. Most important, he thought, she couldn't accuse him of making it up.

Several days had passed and then there was the weekend. Just like back home, weekends meant no school and no work. Michael got up late and helped his sisters clean up their room. Michael's mother had done some laundry in the laundry room and had some clean clothes for Michael to put away. He spent most of the rest of the day with his dad in the hangar. It was nearing the time to leave for home and his dad was getting the plane ready for the trip back. He was helped by Sergeants Campbell and Banks so Michael was mostly just watching.

While he did he started to think. Sometimes his dad said that was dangerous for him to do, but something made him think of the days back at the beginning of this adventure. He remembered one time in a conversation when he was listening to his dad and he said something about them not being able to take the plane and leave when they were in danger.

So he decided to find out why.

"Dad, why couldn't we just leave back when those men were shooting at us?"

"What are you talking about Michael?" His dad said as he worked to put a cover back on the engine.

"You said one day when we first got here and those men were shooting at us that we couldn't just leave. What did you mean?"

"I'm not sure I understand you, I said we couldn't leave?" His dad seemed unaware he had ever said that.

"Yeah, you said we had to stay here."

"Oh I think I remember now, I said we couldn't leave because it would have been dangerous to be taking off and have someone be shooting at us. Also, it takes a couple of days to get this plane ready to fly and we didn't have a couple of days."

"Why does it take so long to get the plane ready?"

"Because it needs to be fueled and then the engines need to be warmed up and the systems checked, before we can take off."

Michael seemed like he understood, his questions had been answered, so he just decided to head back to the room. His mother was getting everything ready to pack for the trip home and he wanted to make sure she had all of his things.

That night at dinner, the group celebrated its work there in the Arctic. They had completed everything they wanted to do and also stopped the destruction of the site. They reflected on all of the events that had happened over the three weeks they were there. It seemed so long ago that the site was in danger of being blown up and now it was a laboratory operating at full speed. Michael's dad explained that another group would be coming in to take over next week and that they had all done a fantastic job of getting the site ready ahead of schedule.

Because it was the final night the adults agreed to allow the children to stay up late and join in a party.

Michael was excited about that, he loved to party. He helped the other kids make some punch out of soda water and some fruit juice mix that they had. Then his dad brought out a big box of frozen food he had stored outside the hangar that no one knew about. It had little pizza rolls, taquitos, ice cream, and even some candy. His dad then told them he saved it for a special occasion and this was it.

Michael's mother was rather shocked that he was able to keep it hidden so long, especially the candy.

They ate, drank, and played music. Some of the kids danced and told jokes. Michael didn't dance, he sat near the wall and looked out at the group. They were singing, dancing, and laughing. He thought about what they had been through and how this could've all been different. He remembered how he felt when the tent exploded and how scared he was. He thought about the Korean soldiers and how scared they must have been.

He looked over at his mother, her face had a smile on it as she watched the children and talked. He thought how sad she would have been had something happened to him. He remembered once again, back to that Christmas Eve, when the music had been playing. He realized what he had heard in the songs that were playing. The Christmas spirit was more than in the giving of gifts, it was the love that we share for each other. He felt that love, for his parents, his sisters, and all of the people who were there with him. He felt the passion his family had for him and his life. He knew he had special powers, powers that would make him different from other kids his age. He now knew what they were.

As he sat there it just came to him. I am special, because

I am loved. The meaning of the word took on a whole new definition to him at this point. He began to understand all of the times that his parents had gotten mad at him for not doing his best in school. He thought it was because they were just mean, but now he knew it was because they cared.

He had a glazed look on his face from thinking so hard about this new found knowledge that he didn't see his dad come over to him.

"What are you thinking about Michael?" His dad inquired.

"Nothing," he said as he looked up at his dad and smiled.

"Well then, what are you grinning at goofy?" His dad asked.

"Oh, I just think it's funny how everyone is dancing." He didn't want to tell his dad that he had figured it out, he couldn't let him know he understood. He figured it would be best just to keep his new knowledge to himself and become the best son he could be.

Chapter 19

MORNING CAME very quickly and the kids were awakened by their parents to prepare for the trip home. It seemed like such a good idea to stay up late last night…, until now.

Michael rolled out of his bed and gathered his things. His mother was standing by to pack his pajamas and take the blankets off the bed. Michelle and Kimberly were also getting up and trying to gather their things. Michael's dad came in and said he needed Michael to come and help him with their bags. Michael was not really thrilled about this, but he dressed quickly and headed into the main room to help. They had everything packed up and ready and his parents were checking around to make sure they had everything.

"Take these bags to the plane and then come back for some more," his dad said to him as he entered the room.

"Dad, I haven't even brushed my teeth yet," Michael said.

"Well go do that and then get in here and take the bags."

Michael rushed off to the bathroom and took care of his business and brushed. His mother came in the middle of him brushing to gather his toothbrush. He was beginning to feel rushed.

He went into the main room and picked up as many bags as he could carry and left for the hangar. When he got there Sergeant Campbell was arranging the luggage on a pallet inside of the plane. He saw Michael and told him to just put them on top and he would take care of them. Michael had a memory of doing this once before. He dropped the bags and headed back to the room for some more. On his way, he passed his dad heading toward the plane with a bag, and his dad said to hurry up because they needed to get going.

Michael could only wonder what the big hurry was, it wasn't as if they were going to miss a plane or something. He got back to the room and the others were all finished cleaning up and had all grabbed some bags. Michael picked up the last two and they all headed out toward the hangar.

He saw Major Daniels walking through the complex, he was shutting down some of the systems. When he saw Michael, Major Daniels said, "Are you ready to go?"

Michael just shook his head yes and said back, "What are you doing?"

"I'm shutting down some of the non-necessary systems in the complex. We are going to put it on minimum power until the other group arrives. It saves on the fuel and generators."

Again, Michael just shook his head like he understood it all. He continued to walk toward the hangar and as he did he had some nice memories of the things he had seen and done here. He passed by the room that had the hole in the wall when they first arrived. He thought about that and how it turned out to not be aliens. He looked out the window and saw the flagpole with the flag on it and remembered his first trip outside and how it was almost his last. As he entered the hangar, he noticed the snowmobiles and thought about the trips on them to the unknown and how things worked out for the best. He smiled and then made his way to the plane.

He put the remaining bags on the plane and then stayed to help Sergeant Campbell tie it all down. He then decided to go and help his dad with the preflight checks and disconnecting the power cable from the plane. He knew all about this now and was pleased with himself that he had remembered and actually learned something. His dad was also pleased and Michael could tell this without him saying. He had a look in his eyes Michael understood, the look of a proud dad.

Everyone was gathered near the plane now and Michael's dad went through the briefing again. He told them that they would pull the plane out of the hangar and onto the snow and ice. They would then start the engines and turn toward the wind and take off. The flight back would follow the same route as the one here and they would be in Greenland in about two hours, depending on the winds.

He instructed everyone to board and buckle up while they got ready to pull the plane out into the cold. Michael helped his sister Kimberly into her seat and strapped her down. He liked helping Kimberly because she always said please and thank you. He took a seat himself, wondering if he was needed outside again.

His mother sat next to him again and Michelle was in the seat on the other side of her. Everyone was in their seats and ready to go. The pilots along with Michael's dad opened the doors to the hangar and using the snowmobiles, pulled the plane out onto the snow and ice. It seemed like it would be impossible for the snowmobiles to do this, but once the plane was moving it was relatively easy to keep it going, and once they were on the ice it was really easy. They felt the plane stop and Michael could see his dad and the others putting the snowmobiles back into the hangar.

They ran onto the plane and closed the door. It was getting rather cold on the plane and everyone was pulling blankets over themselves. It was still dark, had been most of the time they were there and Michael thought he may never see the sun again.

In a brief moment they could hear the engines begin to start. It was like starting an old Dodge on a cold day. Michael's mother could be heard saying a small prayer. Michael just smiled at her thinking she was being funny… She wasn't.

Before long the engines were running and the lights came on. The heat began to flow through the plane. Michael could feel the heat coming from a pipe above his head and it felt nice. He removed the blanket from Kimberly and she smiled at him. The plane then began to move, lumbering through the snow and out away from the buildings. Lucky for everyone his dad had done this before. It was really smooth as they accelerated down the frozen tundra and into the blue, or actually the black.

Michael strained to look out the window and say goodbye to the base, but all he could see was darkness and a bit of snow blowing in the light on the wing. He thought about the flagpole and how he never got to find out if his tongue would stick to it. Never the less, they were on their way home. Home to the house, cars, traffic, sunlight shining in the window, and dare he say, school.

"What a trip," he said out loud, but no one could hear him over the engine noise, and the ear plugs everyone had put in their ears.

He sat back in the seat and closed his eyes. He figured if he slept the trip would go by faster. He tried to sleep, but couldn't. All he could do was think about what he had done and seen on this trip. It was way more than he could ever have imagined.

He leaned over and asked his mom, "Did you have fun?"

"Yes I did Michael," she responded.

"Me too," Michael said with a big smile.

"But it will be nice to get back home and see the sun again, won't it?"

"Yeah and all my friends too."

Michael sat back in his seat and closed his eyes, trying to see if he could sleep. The groan of the engines was all he could hear and before he knew what was happening, he fell asleep. He dreamed of flying again and running in the snow. It was one of those dreams that he would have when he had done the same thing all day and then saw it in his dreams that night. He woke up several times to find the plane still piercing through the dark skies over the top of the world.

Then he felt the plane touch down. He looked over at his mother and was sure she was praying again. She noticed him look at her and said, "Good morning sunshine."

He wiped the drool from his mouth and looked out the

window. There in the window he could actually see blue sky and light.

"Are we home?" He asked.

"Nope, we're in Greenland," his mother answered.

He had slept almost the whole flight. Thankfully, so did Kimberly, which made his nap possible. She would have definitely talked his ear off, had she been awake.

It was basically the same plan as the flight to the Arctic. The stop in Greenland was for fuel and a bite to eat and the kids again played in the snow. This time however, it was sunny and a little bit warmer. It felt so good to feel the sun and all of the children wanted to stay and play. But after a refuel on the plane and their stomachs, it was time to head for Goose Bay again.

On the flight from Greenland to Labrador, which is where Goose Bay was located, Michael sat in the front with his dad. He was familiar with the operation of the flight deck and he again enjoyed just watching the pilots work. He also liked the view from up here. He could see forever in the clear blue sky that they were flying in.

"Isn't it nice to see the sun again?" He asked the pilots.

"Yes it is," they all responded at once.

"But I will miss the base up there," Michael said in a low voice.

His dad turned in his seat and looked at him. He gazed at him for a moment and then said, "Did you really have fun or are you just saying that?"

"I really had fun dad, and I learned so much, so many things about life and everything."

Michael's dad continued to look at him. Michael wasn't sure if he was supposed to say more or if his dad didn't understand him. Then his dad smiled at him and turned around.

As they approached Goose Bay, the sun was far in the western sky. It was nearing night fall on the east coast of Canada. They landed and taxied over to the ramp where they had parked before and everyone got off and went into the building. This time the kids went with the adults. No one was feeling like playing. It was getting late and everyone was very tired.

The kids sat in a room with a TV and for the first time in weeks they watched regular shows. When Michael's dad came in to tell them it was time to go they just sat, fixated on the screen, as if they were in a trance. His dad actually had to walk over in front of the TV to get their attention.

All of the members of the party then reloaded the plane for the last leg of their journey. It was nice to finally be taking off for the last time on this trip. Knowing the next landing, barring any mechanical failures, would be at home.

The final leg took nearly six hours and it was the worst part of the whole trip. The anticipation of going home made it feel so long and grueling. All everyone wanted was to get home and sleep in their own beds.

The landing in Washington was great, all of the adults cheered when the plane touched down. It was late in the night, around midnight and most of the kids were asleep in their seats.

Michael helped the others gather their luggage and things from the plane. There was a van and a driver to take each family home and before they left everyone was walking around, saying goodbye, and hugging. Michael heard his mother setting up times for the group to get together for some cookouts and parties. He thought that would be nice, since he liked everyone who was with them and had so much fun with them. Even though it was so late and he was so tired, he knew he would miss them and his feelings were of sadness that this trip was over.

As Michael stood next to the plane, each member of the crew came over to him and shook his hand. They each said thank you and that they were going to miss him. Michael wasn't sure how to react to this. He was very tired and a bit confused. He realized that his life was going to be different. He just didn't know how to handle that yet.

His family gathered all of their things and got into one of the vans. His dad was the last to leave and had left the plane in the hands of some airmen who were there to greet them. The trip home was quiet, not much traffic and not much talking. They got home to find their house in good shape, a neighbor had been watching it for them and they had left some lights on. There was even a plate of chocolate chip cookies on the counter, she had made for them.

Michael trudged up the steps, went into his room, and crashed on his bed. He could hear his mom and dad putting his sisters in their room and then bringing up their bags. The last thing he remembered before falling asleep was his mother covering him up.

Michael opened his eyes and found he was looking directly into the bright sunlight entering his window. Someone had opened his blind and let it in, but there was no one around. He could smell coffee and hear some talking coming from downstairs. He sat up in his bed and wasn't sure where he was for a minute. He had no idea what time it was.

He made his way downstairs not sure what day it was,

or if he had school. He looked at his parents sitting at the table and they looked back at him. They waited, as he just stood there for a moment.

His dad said, "What…?"

Michael gazed at them with his goofy look. He looked around the kitchen and then with a very confused look said, "You wouldn't believe the dream I just had."

ISBN 141209168-3